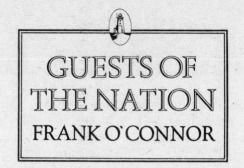

GUESTS OF
THE NATION
FRANK O'CONNOR

D0746747

POOLBEG

Although the theme of the Irish Revolution was to engage Frank O'Connor's attention throughout his life, his first book, *Guests of the Nation,* is his only collection of stories to centre upon it. In it he was concerned with the way in which war imposes a false and cruel ethic on people, implacably destroying human relationships. The title-story itself has been widely acknowledged as one of the greatest anti-war stories ever written, and while, as one critic has put it, "a flippant attitude dominates a few stories in *Guests of the Nation,* a deeper, more substantial note of tragic disaffection moves surely throughout the volume giving the comic stories ironic edge and the tragic stories earnest solemnity."

Frank O'Connor — the pseudonym of Michael O'Donovan — was born in Cork in 1903 and educated there at the Christian Brothers School. He worked as a librarian, first in Co. Cork and then in Dublin. He started writing when very young — commencing a collected edition of his own works when he was twelve — and much of his early poetry, stories and translations was published in AE's *Irish Statesman.* His many collections of short stories — of which *Guests of the Nation* was the first — gained him a world-wide reputation as one of the greatest masters of the form. He died in 1966.

Contents

First published 1931 by
Macmillan & Co., Ltd., London.

First paperback edition published 1979 by
Poolbeg Press Ltd., Knocksedan House,
Swords, Co. Dublin, Ireland.
This edition published 1985.
Reprinted 1987.

Designed by Steven Hope
Cover from *Men of the South*
by Sean Keating (1889-1977),
courtesy of the Crawford Gallery, Cork.

Printed by The Guernsey Press Co. Ltd.,
Vale, Guernsey, Channel Islands.

Guests of the Nation

I

At dusk the big Englishman, Belcher, would shift his long legs out of the ashes and say "Well, chums, what about it?" and Noble and myself would say "All right, chum" (for we had picked up some of their curious expressions), and the little Englishman, Hawkins, would light the lamp and bring out the cards. Sometimes Jeremiah Donovan would come up and supervise the game, and get excited over Hawkins' cards, which he always played badly, and shout at him, as if he was one of our own, "Ah, you divil, why didn't you play the tray?"

But ordinarily Jeremiah was a sober and contented poor devil like the big Englishman, Belcher, and was looked up to only because he was a fair hand at documents, though he was slow even with them. He wore a small cloth hat and big gaiters over his long pants, and you seldom saw him with his hands out of his pockets. He reddened when you talked to him, tilting from toe to heel and back, and looking down all the time at his big farmer's feet. Noble and myself used to make fun of his broad accent, because we were both from the town.

I could not at the time see the point of myself and Noble guarding Belcher and Hawkins at all, for it was my belief that you could have planted that pair down anywhere from this to Claregalway and they'd have taken root there like a native weed. I never in my short experience saw two men take to the country as they did.

They were passed on to us by the Second Battalion

when the search for them became too hot, and Noble and myself, being young, took them over with a natural feeling of responsibility, but Hawkins made us look like fools when he showed that he knew the country better than we did.

"You're the bloke they call Bonaparte," he says to me. "Mary Brigid O'Connell told me to ask what you'd done with the pair of her brother's socks you borrowed."

For it seemed, as they explained it, that the Second had little evenings, and some of the girls of the neighbourhood turned up, and, seeing they were such decent chaps, our fellows could not leave the two Englishmen out. Hawkins learned to dance "The Walls of Limerick", "The Siege of Ennis" and "The Waves of Tory" as well as any of them, though he could not return the compliment, because our lads at that time did not dance foreign dances on principle.

So whatever privileges Belcher and Hawkins had with the Second they just took naturally with us, and after the first couple of days we gave up all pretence of keeping an eye on them. Not that they could have got far, because they had accents you could cut with a knife, and wore khaki tunics and overcoats with civilian pants and boots, but I believe myself they never had any idea of escaping and were quite content to be where they were.

It was a treat to see how Belcher got off with the old woman in the house where we were staying. She was a great warrant to scold, and cranky even with us, but before ever she had a chance of giving our guests, as I may call them, a lick of her tongue, Belcher had made her his friend for life. She was breaking sticks, and Belcher who had not been more than ten minutes in the house, jumped up and went over to her.

"Allow me, madam," he said, smiling his queer little smile. "Please allow me," and he took the hatchet from her. She was too surprised to speak, and after that, Belcher would be at her heels, carrying a bucket, a basket or a load of turf. As Noble said, he got into looking before she leapt, and hot water, or any little thing she wanted, Belcher would have ready for her. For such a huge man (and though I am five foot ten myself I had to look up at him) he had an uncommon lack of speech. It took us a little while to get used to him, walking in and out like a ghost, without speaking. Especially because Hawkins talked enough for a platoon, it was strange to hear Belcher with his toes in the ashes come out with a solitary "Excuse me, chum," or "That's right, chum." His one and only passion was cards, and he was a remarkably good card player. He could have skinned myself and Noble, but whatever we lost to him, Hawkins lost to us, and Hawkins only played with the money Belcher gave him.

Hawkins lost to us because he had too much old gab, and we probably lost to Belcher for the same reason. Hawkins and Noble argued about religion into the early hours of the morning, and Hawkins worried the life out of Noble, who had a brother a priest, with a string of questions that would puzzle a cardinal. Even in treating of holy subjects, Hawkins had a deplorable tongue. I never met a man who could mix such a variety of cursing and bad language into any argument. He was a terrible man, and a fright to argue. He never did a stroke of work, and when he had no one else to argue with, he got stuck in the old woman.

He met his match in her, for when he tried to get her to complain profanely of the drought she gave him a great comedown by blaming it entirely on Jupiter Pluvius (a diety neither Hawkins nor I had ever heard of, though Noble said that among the pagans it was believed that he had something to do with the rain). Another day he was swearing at the capitalists for starting the German war when the old lady laid down her iron, puckered up her little crab's mouth and said: "Mr Hawkins, you can say what you like about the war, and think you'll deceive me because I'm only a simple poor countrywoman, but I know what started the war. It was the Italian Count that stole the heathen divinity out of the temple of Japan. Believe me, Mr. Hawkins, nothing but sorrow and want can follow people who disturb the hidden powers."

A queer old girl, all right.

II

One evening we had our tea and Hawkins lit the lamp and we all sat into cards. Jeremiah Donovan came in too, and sat and watched us for a while, and it suddenly struck me that he had no great love for the two Englishmen. It came as a surprise to me because I had noticed nothing of it before.

Late in the evening a really terrible argument blew up between Hawkins and Noble about capitalists and priests and love of country.

"The capitalists pay the priests to tell you about the next world so that you won't notice what the bastards are up to in this," said Hawkins.

"Nonsense, man!" said Noble, losing his temper. "Before ever a capitalist was thought of people believed in the next world."

Hawkins stood up as though he was preaching.

"Oh, they did, did they?" he said with a sneer. "They believed all the things you believe—isn't that what you mean? And you believe God created Adam, and Adam created Shem, and Shem created Jehoshophat. You believe all that silly old fairytale about Eve and Eden and the apple. Well listen to me, chum! If you're entitled to a silly belief like that, I'm entitled to my own silly belief —which is that the first thing your God created was a bleeding capitalist, with morality and Rolls-Royce complete. Am I right, chum?" he says to Belcher.

"You're right, chum," says Belcher with a smile, and he got up from the table to stretch his long legs into the fire and stroke his moustache. So, seeing that Jeremiah Donovan was going, and that there was no knowing when the argument about religion would be over, I went out with him. We strolled down to the village together, and then he stopped, blushing and mumbling, and said I should be behind, keeping guard. I didn't like the tone he took with me, and anyway I was bored with life in the cottage, so I replied by asking what the hell we wanted to guard them for at all.

He looked at me in surprise and said: "I thought you knew we were keeping them as hostages."

"Hostages?" I said.

"The enemy have prisoners belonging to us, and now they're talking of shooting them," he said. "If they shoot our prisoners, we'll shoot theirs."

"Shoot Belcher and Hawkins?" I said.

"What else did you think we were keeping them for?" he said.

"Wasn't it very unforeseen of you not to warn Noble and myself of that in the beginning?" I said.

"How was it?" he said. "You might have known that much."

"We could not know it, Jeremiah Donovan," I said. "How could we when they were on our hands so long?"

"The enemy have our prisoners as long and longer," he said.

"That's not the same thing at all," said I.

"What difference is there?" said he.

I couldn't tell him, because I knew he wouldn't understand. If it was only an old dog that you had to take to the vet's, you'd try and not get too fond of him, but Jeremiah Donovan was not a man who would ever be in danger of that.

"And when is this to be decided?" I said.

"We might hear tonight," he said. "Or tomorrow or the next day at latest. So if it's only hanging round that's a trouble to you, you'll be free soon enough."

It was not the hanging round that was a trouble to me at all by this time. I had worse things to worry about. When I got back to the cottage the argument was still on. Hawkins was holding forth in his best style, maintaining that there was no next world, and Noble saying that there was; but I could see that Hawkins had had the best of it.

"Do you know what, chum?" he was saying with a saucy smile. "I think you're just as big a bleeding unbeliever as I am. You say you believe in the next world, and you know just as much about the next world as I do, which is sweet damn-all. What's heaven? You don't know. Where's heaven? You don't know. You know sweet damn-all! I ask you again, do they wear wings?"

"Very well, then," said Noble. "They do. Is that enough for you? They do wear wings."

"Where do they get them then? Who makes them? Have they a factory for wings? Have they a sort of store where you hand in your chit and take your bleeding wings?"

"You're an impossible man to argue with," said Noble. "Now, listen to me—" And they were off again.

It was long after midnight when we locked up and went to bed. As I blew out the candle I told Noble. He took it very quietly. When we'd been in bed about an hour he asked if I thought we should tell the Englishmen. I didn't, because I doubted if the English would shoot our men. Even if they did, the Brigade officers, who were always up and down to the Second Battalion and knew the Englishmen well, would hardly want to see them plugged. "I think so too," said Noble. "It would be great cruelty to put the wind up them now."

"It was very unforeseen of Jeremiah Donovan, anyhow," said I.

It was next morning that we found it so hard to face Belcher and Hawkins. We went about the house all day, scarcely saying a word. Belcher didn't seem to notice; he was stretched into the ashes as usual, with his usual look of waiting in quietness for something unforeseen to happen, but Hawkins noticed it and put it down to Noble being beaten in the argument of the night before.

"Why can't you take the discussion in the proper spirit?" he said severely. "You and your Adam and Eve! I'm a Communist, that's what I am. Communist or

Anarchist, it all comes to much the same thing." And he went round the house, muttering when the fit took him: "Adam and Eve! Adam and Eve! Nothing better to do with their time than pick bleeding apples!"

III

I don't know how we got through that day, but I was very glad when it was over, the tea things were cleared away, and Belcher said in his peaceable way: "Well, chums, what about it?" We sat round the table and Hawkins took out the cards, and just then I heard Jeremiah Donovan's footsteps on the path and a dark presentiment crossed my mind. I rose from the table and caught him before he reached the door.

"What do you want?" I asked.

"I want those two soldier friends of yours," he said, getting red.

"Is that the way, Jeremiah Donovan?" I asked.

"That s the way. There were four of our lads shot this morning, one of them a boy of sixteen."

"That's bad," I said.

At that moment Noble followed me out, and the three of us walked down the path together, talking in whispers. Feeney, the local intelligence officer, was standing by the gate.

"What are you going to do about it?" I asked Jeremiah Donovan.

"I want you and Noble to get them out; tell them they're being shifted again; that'll be the quietest way."

"Leave me out of that," said Noble, under his breath.

Jeremiah Donovan looked at him hard.

"All right," he says. "You and Feeney get a few tools from the shed and dig a hole by the far end of the bog. Bonaparte and myself will be after you. Don't let anyone see you with the tools. I wouldn't like it to go beyond ourselves."

We saw Feeney and Noble go round to the shed and went in ourselves. I left Jeremiah Donovan to do the explanations. He told them that he had orders to send them back to the Second Battalion. Hawkins let out a mouthful of curses, and you could see that though Belcher didn't say anything, he was a bit upset too. The old woman was for having them stay in spite of us, and she didn't stop advising them until Jeremiah Donovan lost his temper and turned on her. He had a nasty temper, I noticed. It was pitch dark in the cottage by this time, but no one thought of lighting the lamp, and in the darkness the two Englishmen fetched their topcoats and said good-bye to the old woman.

"Just as a man makes a home of a bleeding place, some bastard at headquarters thinks you're too cushy and shunts you off," said Hawkins, shaking her hand.

"A thousand thanks, madam," said Belcher. "A thousand thanks for everything"—as though he'd made it up.

We went round to the back of the house and down towards the bog. It was only then that Jeremiah Donovan told them. He was shaking with excitement.

"There were four of our fellows shot in Cork this morning and now you are to be shot as a reprisal."

"What are you talking about?" snaps Hawkins. "It's bad enough being mucked about as we are without having to put up with your funny jokes."

"It isn't a joke," said Donovan. "I'm sorry, Hawkins, but it's true," and begins on the usual rigmarole about duty and how unpleasant it is. I never noticed that people who talk a lot about duty find it much of a trouble to them.

"Oh, cut it out!" said Hawkins.

"Ask Bonaparte," said Donovan, seeing that Hawkins wasn't taking him seriously. "Isn't it true, Bonaparte?"

"It is," I said, and Hawkins stopped.

"Ah, for Christ's sake, chum!"

"I mean it, chum," I said.

"You don't sound as if you meant it."

"If he doesn't mean it, I do," said Donovan, working himself up.

"What have you against me, Jeremiah Donovan?"

"I never said I had anything against you. But why did your people take out four of your prisoners and shoot them in cold blood?"

He took Hawkins by the arm and dragged him on, but it was impossible to make him understand that we were in earnest. I had the Smith and Wesson in my pocket and I kept fingering it and wondering what I'd do if they put up a fight for it or ran, and wishing to God they'd do one or the other. I knew if they did run for it, that I'd never fire on them. Hawkins wanted to know was Noble in it, and when we said yes, he asked us why Noble wanted to plug him. Why did any of us want to plug him? What had he done to us? Weren't we all chums? Didn't we understand him and didn't he understand us? Did we imagine for an instant that he'd shoot us for all the so-and-so officers in the so-and-so British Army?

By this time we'd reached the bog, and I was so sick I couldn't even answer him. We walked along the edge of it in the darkness, and every now and then Hawkins would call a halt and begin all over again, as if he was wound up, about our being chums, and I knew that nothing but the sight of the grave would convince him that we had to do it. And all the time I was hoping that something would happen; that they'd run for it or that Noble would take over the responsibility from me. I had the feeling that it was worse on Noble than on me.

IV

At last we saw the lantern in the distance and made towards it. Noble was carrying it, and Feeney was standing somewhere in the darkness behind him, and the picture of them so still and silent in the bogland brought it home to me that we were in earnest, and banished the last bit of hope I had.

Belcher, on recognising Noble, said: "Hallo, chum," in

his quiet way, but Hawkins flew at him at once, and the argument began all over again, only this time Noble had nothing to say for himself and stood with his head down, holding the lantern between his legs.

It was Jeremiah Donovan who did the answering. For the twentieth time, as though it was haunting his mind, Hawkins asked if anybody thought he'd shoot Noble.

"Yes, you would," said Jeremiah Donovan.

"No, I wouldn't, damn you!"

"You would, because you'd know you'd be shot for not doing it."

"I wouldn't, not if I was to be shot twenty times over. I wouldn't shoot a pal. And Belcher wouldn't—isn't that right, Belcher?"

"That's right, chum," Belcher said, but more by way of answering the question than of joining in the argument. Belcher sounded as though whatever unforeseen thing he'd always been waiting for had come at last.

"Anyway, who says Noble would be shot if I wasn't? What do you think I'd do if I was in his place, out in the middle of a blasted bog?"

"What would you do?" asked Donovan.

"I'd go with him wherever he was going, of course. Share my last bob with him and stick by him through thick and thin. No one can ever say of me that I let down a pal."

"We've had enough of this," said Jeremiah Donovan, cocking his revolver. "Is there any message you want to send?"

"No, there isn't."

"Do you want to say your prayers?"

Hawkins came out with a cold-blooded remark that even shocked me and turned on Noble again.

"Listen to me Noble," he said. "You and me are chums. You can't come over to my side, so I'll come over to your side. That show you I mean what I say? Give me a rifle and I'll go along with you and the other lads."

Noble answered him. We knew that was no way out.

"Hear what I'm saying?" he said. "I'm through with it.

I'm a deserter or anything else you like. I don't believe in your stuff, but it's no worse than mine. That satisfy you?"

Noble raised his head, but Donovan began to speak and he lowered it again without replying.

"For the last time, have you any messages to send?" said Donovan in a cold, excited sort of voice.

"Shut up, Donovan! You don't understand me, but these lads do. They're not the sort to make a pal and kill a pal. They're not the tools of any capitalist."

I alone of the crowd saw Donovan raise his Webley to the back of Hawkins's neck, and as he did so I shut my eyes and tried to pray. Hawkins had begun to say something else when Donovan fired, and as I opened my eyes at the bang, I saw Hawkins stagger at the knees and lie out flat at Noble's feet, slowly and as quiet as a kid falling asleep, with the lanternlight on his lean legs and bright farmer's boots. We all stood very still, watching him settle out in the last agony.

Then Belcher took out a hankerchief and began to tie it about his own eyes (in our excitement we'd forgotten to do the same for Hawkins), and, seeing it wasn't big enough, turned and asked for the loan of mine. I gave it to him, and he knotted the two together and pointed with his foot at Hawkins.

"He's not quite dead," he said. "Better give him another."

Sure enough, Hawkins's left knee was beginning to rise. I bent down and put my gun to his head; then recollecting myself, I got up again. Belcher understood what was in my mind.

"Give him his first," he said. "I don't mind. Poor bastard, we don't know what's happening to him now."

I knelt and fired. By this time I didn't seem to know what I was doing. Belcher, who was fumbling a bit awkwardly with the handkerchiefs, came out with a laugh as he heard the shot. It was the first time I had heard him laugh and it sent a shudder down my back; it sounded so unnatural.

"Poor bugger!" he said quietly. "And last night he was so curious about it all. It's very queer, chums, I always think. Now he knows as much about it as they'll ever let him know, and last night he was all in the dark."

Donovan helped him to tie the handkerchiefs about his eyes. "Thanks, chum," he said. Donovan asked if there were any messages he wanted sent.

"No, chum," he said. "Not for me. If any of you would like to write to Hawkins's mother, you'll find a letter from her in his pocket. He and his mother were great chums. But my missus left me eight years ago. Went away with another fellow and took the kid with her. I like the feeling of a home, as you may have noticed, but I couldn't start another again after that."

It was an extraordinary thing, but in those few minutes Belcher said more than in all the weeks before. It was just as if the sound of the shot had started a flood of talk in him and he could go on the whole night like that, quite happily, talking about himself. We stood around like fools now that he couldn't see us any longer. Donovan looked at Noble, and Noble shook his head. Then Donovan raised his Webley, and at that moment Belcher gave his queer laugh again. He may have thought we were talking about him, or perhaps he noticed the same thing I'd noticed and couldn't understand it.

"Excuse me, chums," he said. "I feel I'm talking the hell of a lot, and so silly, about my being so handy about a house and things like that. But this thing came on me suddenly. You'll forgive me, I'm sure."

"You don't want to say a prayer?" asked Donovan.

"No, chum," he said. "I don't think it would help. I'm ready, and you boys want to get it over."

"You understand that we're only doing our duty?" said Donovan.

Belcher's head was raised like a blind man's, so that you could only see his chin and the top of his nose in the lantern-light.

"I never could make out what duty was myself," he

16

said. "I think you're all good lads, if that's what you mean. I'm not complaining."

Noble, just as if he couldn't bear any more of it, raised his fist at Donovan, and in a flash Donovan raised his gun and fired. The big man went over like a sack of meal, and this time there was no need for a second shot.

I don't remember much about the burying, but that it was worse than all the rest because we had to carry them to the grave. It was all mad lonely with nothing but a patch of lantern-light between ourselves and the dark, and birds hooting and screeching all round, disturbed by the guns. Noble went through Hawkins's belongings to find the letter from his mother, and then joined his hands together. He did the same with Belcher. Then, when we'd filled in the grave, we separated from Jeremiah Donovan and Feeney and took our tools back to the shed. All the way we didn't speak a word. The kitchen was dark and cold as we'd left it, and the old woman was sitting over the hearth, saying her beads. We walked past her into the room, and Noble struck a match to light the lamp. She rose quietly and came to the doorway with all her cantankerousness gone.

"What did ye do with them?" she asked in a whisper, and Noble started so that the match went out in his hand.

"What's that?" he asked without turning round.

"I heard ye," she said.

"What did you hear?" asked Noble.

"I heard ye. Do you think I didn't hear ye, putting the spade back in the houseen?"

Noble struck another match and this time the lamp lit for him.

"Was that what ye did to them?" she asked.

Then, by God, in the very doorway, she fell on her knees and began praying, and after looking at her for a minute or two Noble did the same by the fireplace. I pushed my way out past her and left them at it. I stood at the door, watching the stars and listening to the shrieking of the birds dying out over the bogs. It is so strange what

17

you feel at times like that that you can't describe it. Noble says he saw everything ten times the size, as though there were nothing in the whole world but that little patch of bog with the two Englishmen stiffening into it, but with me it was as if the patch of bog where the Englishmen were was a million miles away, and even Noble and the old woman, mumbling behind me, and the birds and the bloody stars were all far away, and I was somehow very small and very lost and lonely like a child astray in the snow. And anything that happened to me afterwards, I never felt the same about again.

Attack

Lomasney and I came through the wood after dark, and at the stepping-stones over the little stream we were joined by another man who carried a carbine in the crook of his arm. We went on in silence, Lomasney leading the way across the sodden, slippery ground.

The attack on the barrack was timed to begin at two hours after midnight, and as yet it was only nine o'clock. Beneath us, through the trees, we could see a solitary light burning in one of the barrack bedrooms where some thoughtless policeman had forgotten to close the shutters. Surrounded by barbed wire, its windows shuttered with steel, the old building stood on the outskirts of the village, a formidable nut to crack.

But for a long time now this attack of ours was being promised to the garrison, whose sense of duty had outrun their common sense. Policemen are like that. A soldier never does more than he need do, and so far as possible he keeps on good terms with his enemy; for him the ideal is the least amount of disorder; he only asks not to be taken prisoner or ambushed or blown up too often. But for the policeman there is only one ideal, Order, hushed and entire; to his well-drilled mind a stray shot at a rabbit and a stray shot at a general are one and the same thing, so that in civil commotion he loses all sense of proportion and becomes a helpless, hopeless, gibbering maniac whom in everybody's interests it is better to remove. That at least was how we thought in those days, and the garrison I speak of had been a bad lot, saucy to the villagers and a nuisance to our men for miles around. Oh, it was coming to them—everybody knew that. In the evenings when the policemen were standing outside their door, sunning themselves and enjoying a smoke; some child's voice would be raised from a distance, singing:

Do you want your old barracks blown down,
  blown down?
Do you want your old barracks blown down?

And blown down it would be if Lomasney's new-fangled explosive that was to put T.N.T. in the shade proved a success.

We jumped the fence above the wood and landed in a meadow whose long, wet grass spread a summery fragrance about us. A star or two shone out above the hill, but night was not yet complete. Lomasney let the other man take the lead and waited for me.

"There's something I wanted to say to you, Owen," he said. "This house we're going to—there's only an old couple in it. They've had a deal of trouble already, and I'd be sorry to frighten them. So I'll let on we're only sheltering for a few hours, and do you make a joke of it if you can."

I agreed, and went on with him in silence, waiting for the explanation that I knew was coming. Lomasney was intense and slow, and you could feel a story or a retort springing up in him long before it passed his lips.

"I've known those people since I was a kid," he went on. "I used to be friendly with the son of the house one time—he was a deal older than I was, but we hit it off well together. He was a big, handsome, devil-may-care fellow, a great favourite with the girls and a fright to hurl. Everybody was fond of him. He was kept down at home by his father, and so he used to spend his evenings anywhere but at home. He'd walk in on top of you, and sit by the fire as if he was one of the family, and, as soon as not, if you'd a bed to spare he'd spend the night with you.

"Five years ago he got into trouble. He was keen on a girl in the village. She was married to a waster who used to beat her. One night her husband was knocked out in a row and didn't over it. Paddy hit him, of course, but it was his head cracking off the floor that did for him. Nobody was very sorry for him, but everybody was sorry for Paddy and the girl.

"That night some of Paddy's friends drove him into the city. The people around vere very decent; they made up enough money to take him to the States, and he cleared out. It was a stupid thing to do—I know that now—but we were frightened of the law in those days.

"Well, since that night there hasn't been tale nor tiding of him. For a while the old father—he has the devil's own pride—was pretending he got letters through boys that had been with Paddy in New York. Maybe he did, in the beginning, but that was as much as he got. To my own knowledge, Paddy never wrote as much as one line home, and the best we can hope for is that he didn't go the same way as some of the others go. I think he must be dead, and things being as they are, I'd rather he was dead. But you can't convince his father of that. He's as certain as the day that Paddy's alive and flourishing, and it would be as much as your life was worth to contradict him."

I was strangely moved by this little tale, mostly I think because it came to divert my thoughts from the dark building below to the cottage up the hill.

The man who accompanied us lifted a heavy branch out of a gateway, we pushed it home again, skirted a field of potatoes, and approached the house from the back. Lomasney knocked, and the door was opened by a sharp-eyed ragged old man whose body was twisted like an apple-tree. He started back when he saw the three of us standing there with our rifles, and let the latch drop with a clatter. Lomasney immediately hailed him in a purposely boisterous tone—too boisterous, I thought, considering our errand, but it had its effect. With a curious gesture he bent forward and drew us in one by one by the hand, giving us as he did so a piercing look that made me wonder if there wasn't a streak of insanity in him. When he took my hand in one of his own old rocky hands and rested the other on my shoulder I felt I understood Lomasney's phrase about contradicting him. There was danger there.

We took our places on a settle beside the fire, opposite an old woman who called out a cracked greeting, but kept her eyes turned away. She wore a black shawl about her shoulders and hair, and her profile was taut in the firelight. The old man lit the lamp. There was a ladder leading to an attic in the centre of the floor, and he took his stand against this, with hands in the pockets of his trousers. He stared at us all in turn, but I came in for the most careful survey. Lomasney made up some legend about me to content the boundless countryman's curiosity in him, and meanwhile, without raising my eyes, I studied him. He was much taller than I had thought him bent beneath the shadow of the doorway, taller and more powerful, with a stubborn and avaricious mouth. His trousers, without as much as a button down the front of it, was in rags, and he hitched it up about his belly with a shrug that displayed the great shoulder-blades and the twisted muscles of his neck. He had a little yellow goat's beard that grew outwards from his chin and made his head appear to be tilted up.

After he had looked his fill at us, he spat out, heaved a chair across to the fire and sat down, spreading his dung-caked legs wide across the hearth.

"'Tis late ye're stopping from yeer homes," he said sourly.

"We've no choice in that," replied Lomasney.

"'Tis late—and foolish."

"Maybe 'tis."

"'Tis."

"We've our work to do," added Lomasney cheerfully.

"Work?" The old man looked at him in pretended wonder. "Work? Oh, ay." He slowly quoted two lines of an Irish song. I saw the old woman's shawled head go up with a little jerk. It was her way of smiling at the aptness of it. But Lomasney and the other man looked blank. The old man bent across and laid a stony hand heavily on Lomasney's knee.

Tramping the dews in the morning airley,

And gathering chills for a quarter. . . .
he translated.

"If we are, there's more like us," said Lomasney, trying to steer the conservation round to politics.

"Wisha, is there?"

"There is, and no one knows that better than yourself, Mike."

I was amused to see the old man dodging him with a very cleverly assumed ignorance or indifference. After a time I saw that he had long since taken the measure of Lomasney's very earnest and passionate but simple mind, and was getting great enjoyment out of the battle of wits. He dropped his air of boorishness, and a glint of sour amusement flickered in his eyes. A bitter remark or two in Irish flung at his wife showed me the measure of his contempt for the younger man. I let him continue this country sport for a while until I saw Lomasney grow confused. Then I threw in a phrase of my own in Irish to show the old rascal that I understood. At this he looked me up and down wonderingly for a moment, broke into a loud, tempestuous laugh, and shoved back his seat to the table.

"Come, woman!" he shouted. "Supper! Supper! The young cock is crowing."

I felt in my heart that he despised me for an interfering young fool.

The old woman filled us out each a jam-crock of milk and cut us a slice of cake. We talked no more during the meal, and when it was over old Kieran produced his beads and knelt beside a chair, touching his forehead with the crucifix. We knelt likewise, all but the old woman, "whose kneecaps were wake," she said. Kieran gave out the rosary.

When the prayers proper were finished Lomasney blessed himself hurriedly and half rose, but the old man's voice, angry and strident, broke in to stop him.

". . . And for my son, Patrick Kieran, who is in the States these five years, Our Father who art in heaven . . ."

And he led us through seven Our Fathers and Hail

Marys before he raised the cross on his beads to bless himself.

When he rose his face was flushed, and the same angry, resentful look was on it that it had worn when he opened the door to us.

"I'm sorry," said Lomasney mildly. I forgot about Patrick."

"Remember him in future," Kieran said churlishly.

"Have you heard from him lately?" Lomasney asked in the same tone.

"What's that to you, young man?" Kieran shouted with sudden fury, showing his bare yellow gums.

"Oh, nothing, nothing. Don't eat us! I only wondered how he was getting on."

"He's getting on—he's getting on all right, never fear. He's in Butte, Montana, now in case you want to know."

"Oh, very well!"

"Why did you ask?"

"Why wouldn't I ask? Wasn't he a friend of mine, man?"

"He have the Son of God to look after him!"

The cry sounded impious, more a challenge than an act of faith.

"Ttttttt!" the old woman sighed moodily into the fire, and Lomasney said no more. Kieran lit a candle and opened the door of a room off the kitchen.

"Stop in there, will ye?"

"We'll be going before morning. We may as well stay in the kitchen."

"Do what ye're toult, man. There's a fine big bed in there ye can all lie on."

There was no mistaking the resentment in his tone, and I nudged Lomasney to let him have his way. Having warned him to leave the front door unbolted, we said good night and went into the room. The third man and I removed our boots and lay down, while Lomasney, who had opened the window, sat on a chair beside us and lit a cigarette. The night was calm and clear. Lomasney looked at his watch.

"Midnight," he said. "They're cutting the wires now. You fellows may as well try and get an hour's sleep. Will I quench that candle?"

He did so. After a little while he continued softly, to me.

"There! What did I tell you? That old fellow is a devil! . . . You're lying on Patrick's bed now. They keep it made up in case he'd come back without warning—and it's shown to everybody who comes inside the door. . . . A queer old pair! . . . And they say the same blessed prayers still! I'd forgotten they'd be doing that."

"They are a queer pair," I said. "The old woman looks as if she was crushed."

"So well she might be."

"And hopeless!"

"Patrick would have been crushed too if he'd stayed at home," Lomasney added, as if he had thought of it for the first time.

After that it was silence. The lad beside me was asleep, as I soon knew by his regular breathing. Lomasney's cigarette died out, and for close on an hour the two of us remained alone with our thoughts. Once we heard a distant explosion that reminded us sharply of the men who had been out since midnight, felling trees and destroying bridges. I thought of the policemen below listening to that, poor devils! Already they probably knew there was something in the wind, and were padding around half-dressed in their slippers, erecting a barricade behind the doors, and asking one another whether they could hold out till morning.

At last, able to bear it no longer, I rose, and stood beside Lomasney, who was leaning with his two elbows on the window-sill, looking down at the little village in the darkness of its valley. His watch lay before him on the window-sill, loudly and petulantly ticking the moments away, and his fingers were drumming a tattoo on the sill. I saw that the barrack was in total darkness. Lomasney told me in a whisper that there had been four lights on top of the building. All had gone out together. Someone must have heard the explosion and tried to phone.

"For God's sake, let's get outside for a bit," he said with ill-suppressed excitement. "I'm suffocating in here."

We tiptoed to the door and opened it softly. Suddenly he caught my arm and drew me back, but not before I had seen something that startled me far more than his gesture. As I have said there was a ladder in the centre of the kitchen, and it gave access to a loft. Now the trap-door that covered the top of the ladder was open and a light was showing through, but even as we looked, it was closed with the utmost care, and the kitchen was in darkness again.

I could feel the excitement of the chase working in Lomasney; his hand twitched against my arm. Then he made a bound for the ladder. It shook under his weight with a squeak; the old woman's voice from another room was suddenly raised in bitter protest, and—I leaped after him.

I can still see myself with my head through that trap and Lomasney standing above me with a drawn revolver. We must have looked a rare pair of grotesques in the light of the candle that old Kieran was holding—on the defensive too, for if ever there was murder in a man's eyes there was murder in his. But what drew our attention was not he, it was the figure that lay on the straw at his feet. Bearded, emaciated, half-savage; this strange creature was lying sideways, his body propped on two spindly arms, staring dully up at us. He wore only a shirt and trousers.

We must have been staring at one another like this for some time before Lomasney seemed to become conscious of the old woman's shrill crying below. To add to the confusion our companion was awake and shouting hysterically at me from the foot of the ladder.

"Go down and stop that woman crying," said Lomasney harshly.

Old Kieran looked as though he would resist, but Lomasney stared coldly past him, pocketed his revolver, and knelt beside the man on the straw. The old man laid his candle on the dresser. I made way for him, and he climbed heavily down the ladder, without as much as a backward glance. I heard him talking to the other man, his voice charged with rage, but I did not catch what he was saying. I had eyes and ears only for what was going on in the loft. I noticed even the heap of weekly papers on the floor and the three or four child's games like "Ludo" and "Snakes and Ladders" beside them.

"You'd better come down too, Paddy," said Lomasney gently.

I ran to help him lift young Kieran, but he waved us both aside and feebly rose without our assistance.

"Have you been here always?" asked Lomasney. "All these long years?" but again the other man just waved his hands, vaguely, as though begging us not to force speech from him.

"Poor devil!" said Lomasney with an anguish of compassion. "Poor devil! If only I'd known it!"

I took hold of his legs and Lomasney of one arm as we helped him down the ladder to the kitchen. A candle was lighting on the mantelpiece, and the old man, his face and beard thrown into startling relief, was sitting with his back to the ladder, glaring at the ashen heap of burnt turf on the hearth. He said nothing, but the boy's mother, who wore an old coat over her nightdress, held out her bare arms and raised a piercing screech when she saw him. We put him sitting beside her on the settle, and she dropped into a quiet moaning, holding his two hands in hers and caressing them tenderly.

Lomasney jerked the old man's shoulder, and anger and contempt mingled in his voice when he spoke.

"Listen to me now," he said. "I'm taking charge here from this on. And I want no more of your cleverness, understand that! You've been too clever too long, confound you, and now you're going to do what I say. . . .

"In two or three days' time you'll go to the city with Patrick. You'll leave him there, and come home without being seen. After that he can come back whenever he pleases—from America that is. We won't say anything

27

about it, and you won't say anything about it, and so far as anybody will know, he will have come from America. Do you understand me?"

"And the policemin?" asked old Kieran sullenly, after a moment's silence. "How long do you think they'll leave him here? Hey."

"Tomorrow," said Lomasney, "there won't be any policemen there, please God!"

Kieran started. He glanced from Lomasney to me and back again. A look, half cunning, half triumph, stole into his bitter old face.

"So that's what he's here for?" he asked, pointing at me. "That's what ye're out for? Do you tell me you're out to ind them? Do you?"

"That's what we're out for," Lomasney answered coldly, fetching his rifle and swinging it across his shoulder.

Kieran chuckled, and the chuckle seemed to shake the whole crazy scaffolding of his bones.

"And I thinking ye were only like children playmaking!" he went on. "Do it, do it, and remember I'll be on me bended knees praying to Almighty God for ye. Divil a wink I'll sleep this night!"

We left them, old Kieran, who seemed to be possessed of a new lease of life, grown garrulous and maddeningly friendly; the mother sitting very quietly beside her son, who had not as much as opened his mouth but down whose beard the heavy, silent tears were rolling as he gazed vacantly at the candle flame.

Lomasney's voice was exultant as we strode down the fields and picked our way through the wood to join the rest of the attacking party who were assembling in the village street from every house around.

"Lord, O Lord!" he exclaimed gleefully, nipping my arm with his fingers. "I never went out on a job with a clearer conscience!"

And a few moments later he added:

"But old Mike Kieran isn't quit of me yet, Owen—damn me but he isn't quit of me yet! I'm a bad judge, Owen, if we haven't signed on our best recruit!"

Jumbo's Wife

I

When he had taken his breakfast, silently as his way was
after a drunk, he lifted the latch and went out without a
word. She heard his feet tramp down the flagged laneway,
waking iron echoes, and, outraged, shook her fist after
him; then she pulled off the old red flannel petticoat and
black shawl she was wearing, and crept back into the hollow of the bed. But not to sleep. She went over and over
in her mind the shame of last night's bout, felt at her lip
where he had split it with a blow, and recalled how she
had fled into the roadway screaming for help and been
brought back by Pa Kenefick, the brother of the murdered
boy. Somehow that had sobered Jumbo. Since Michael,
the elder of the Kenefick brothers, had been taken out and
killed by the police, the people had looked up to Pa as they
looked up to the priest, but more passionately, more
devotedly. She remembered how even Jumbo, the great
swollen insolent Jumbo had crouched back into the
darkness when he saw that slip of a lad walk in before her.
"Stand away from me," he had said, but not threateningly.
"It was a shame," Pa had retorted, "a confounded shame
for a drunken elephant of a man to beat his poor decent
wife like that," but Jumbo had said nothing, only "Let her
be, boy, let her be! Go away from me now and I'll quieten
down." "You'd better quieten down," Pa had said, "or
you'll answer for it to me, you great bully you," and he
had kicked about the floor the pieces of the delf that Jumbo
in his drunken frenzy had shattered one by one against the

wall. "I tell you I won't lay a finger on her," Jumbo had said, and sure enough, when Pa Kenefick had gone, Jumbo was a quiet man.

But it was the sight of the brother of the boy that had been murdered rather than the beating she had had or the despair at seeing her little share of delf smashed on her, that brought home to Jumbo's wife her own utter humiliation. She had often thought before that she would run away from Jumbo, even, in her wild way, that she would do for him, but never before had she seen so clearly what a wreck he had made of her life. The sight of Pa had reminded her that she was no common trollop but a decent girl; he had said it, "your decent poor wife," that was what Pa had said, and it was true; she was a decent poor woman. Didn't the world know how often she had pulled the little home together on her blackguard of a husband, the man who had 'listed in the army under a false name so as to rob her of the separation money, the man who would keep a job only as long as it pleased him, and send her out then to work in the nurseries, picking fruit for a shilling a day?

She was so caught up into her own bitter reflections that when she glanced round suddenly and saw the picture that had been the ostensible cause of Jumbo's fury awry, the glass smashed in it, and the bright colours stained with tea, her lip fell, and she began to moan softly to herself. It was a beautiful piece—that was how she described it—a beautiful, massive piece of a big, big castle, all towers, on a rock, and mountains and snow behind. Four shillings and sixpence it had cost her in the Coal Quay market. Jumbo would spend three times that on a drunk; ay, three times and five times that Jumbo would spend, and for all, he had smashed every cup and plate and dish in the house on her poor little picture—because it was extravagance, he said.

She heard the postman's loud double knock, and the child beside her woke and sat up. She heard a letter being slipped under the door. Little Johnny heard it too. He climbed down the side of the bed, pattered across the floor in his nightshirt and brought it to her. A letter with the

On-His-Majesty's-Service stamp; it was Jumbo's pension that he drew every quarter. She slipped it under her pillow with a fresh burst of rage. It would keep. She would hold on to it until he gave her his week's wages on Friday. Yes, she would make him hand over every penny of it even if he killed her after. She had done it before, and would do it again.

Little Johnny began to cry that he wanted his breakfast, and she rose, sighing, and dressed. Over the fire as she boiled the kettle she meditated again on her wrongs, and was startled when she found the child actually between her legs holding out the long envelope to the flames, trying to boil the kettle with it. She snatched it wildly from his hand and gave him a vicious slap across the face that set him howling. She stood turning the letter over and over in her hand curiously, and then started as she remembered that it wasn't until another month that Jumbo's pension fell due. She counted the weeks; no, that was right, but what had them sending out Jumbo's pension a month before it was due?

When the kettle boiled she made the tea, poured it out into two tin ponnies, and sat into table with the big letter propped up before her as though she was trying to read its secrets through the manilla covering. But she was no closer to solving the mystery when her breakfast of bread and tea was done, and, sudden resolution coming to her, she held the envelope over the spout of the kettle and slowly steamed its fastening away. She drew out the flimsy note inside and opened it upon the table. It was an order, a money order, but not the sort they sent to Jumbo. The writing on it meant little to her, but what did mean a great deal were the careful figures, a two and a five that filled one corner. A two and a five and a sprawling sign before them; this was not for Jumbo—or was it? All sorts of suspicions began to form in her mind, and with them a feeling of pleasurable excitement.

She thought of Pa Kenefick. Pa was a good scholar and the proper man to see about a thing like this. And Pa had been good to her. Pa would feel she was doing the right thing in showing him this mysterious paper, even if it meant nothing but a change in the way they paid Jumbo's pension; it would show how much she looked up to him.

She threw her old black shawl quickly about her shoulders and grabbed at the child's hand. She went down the low arched laneway where they lived—Melancholy Lane, it was called—and up the road to the Kenefick's. She knocked at their door, and Mrs. Kenefick, whose son had been dragged to his death from that door, answered it. She looked surprised when she saw the other woman, and only then Jumbo's wife realised how early it was. She asked excitedly for Pa. He wasn't at home, his mother said, and she didn't know when he would be home, if he came at all. When she saw how crestfallen her visitor looked at this, she asked politely if she couldn't send a message, for women like Jumbo's wife frequently brought information that was of use to the volunteers. No, no, the other woman said earnestly, it was for Pa's ears, for Pa's ears alone, and it couldn't wait. Mrs. Kenefick asked her into the parlour, where the picture of the murdered boy, Michael, in his Volunteer uniform hung. It was dangerous for any of the company to stay at home, she said, the police knew the ins and outs of the district too well; there was the death of Michael unaccounted for, and a dozen or more arrests, all within a month or two. But she had never before seen Jumbo's wife in such a state and wondered what was the best thing for her to do. It was her daughter who decided it by telling where Pa was to be found, and immediately the excited woman raced off up the hill towards the open country.

She knocked at the door of a little farmhouse off the main road, and when the door was opened she saw Pa himself, in shirt-sleeves, filling out a basin of hot water to shave. His first words showed that he thought it was Jumbo who had been at her again, but, without answering him, intensely conscious of herself and of the impression she wished to create, she held the envelope out at arm's length. He took it, looked at the address for a moment, and then pulled out the flimsy slip. She saw his brows bent above it, then his lips tightened. He raised his head and called "Jim, Liam, come down! Come down a minute!" The tone in which he said it delighted her as much as the rush of footsteps upstairs. Two men descended a ladder to the kitchen, and Pa held out the slip. "Look at this!" he said. They looked at it, for a long time it seemed to her, turning it round and round and examining the postmark on the envelope. She began to speak rapidly. "Mr. Kenefick will tell you, gentlemen, Mr. Kenefick will tell you, the life he leads me. I was never one for regulating me own, gentlemen, but I say before me God this minute, hell will never be full till they have him roasting there. A little pitcher I bought gentlemen, a massive little piece – Mr. Kenefick will tell you – I paid four and sixpence for it – he said I was extravagant. Let me remark he'd spend three times, ay, and six times, as much on filling his own gut as I'd spend upon me home and child. Look at me, gentlemen, look at me lip where he hit me – Mr. Kenefick will tell you – I was in gores of blood."

"Listen now, ma'am," one of the men interrupted suavely, "we're very grateful to you for showing us this letter. It's something we wanted to know this long time, ma'am. And now like a good woman will you go back home and not open your mouth to a soul about it, and, if himself ask you anything, say there did ne'er a letter come?" Of course, she said, she would do whatever they told her. She was in their hands. Didn't Mr. Kenefick come in, like the lovely young man he was, and save her from the hands of that dancing hangman Jumbo? And wasn't she sorry for his mother, poor little 'oman, and her fine son taken away on her? Weren't they all crazy about her?

The three men had to push her out the door, saying that she had squared her account with Jumbo at last.

At noon with the basket of food under her arm, and the child plodding along beside her, she made her way through the northern slums to a factory on the outskirts of the city. There, sitting on the grass beside a little stream – her usual station – she waited for Jumbo. He came just as the siren blew, sat down beside her on the grass, and, without as much as fine day, began to unpack the food in the little basket. Already she was frightened and unhappy; she dreaded what Jumbo would do if ever he found out about the letter, and find out he must. People said he wouldn't last long on her, balloon and all as he was. Some said his heart was weak, and others that he was bloated out with dropsy and would die in great agony at any minute. But those who said that hadn't felt the weight of Jumbo's hand.

She sat in the warm sun, watching the child dabble his fingers in the little stream, and all the bitterness melted away within her. She had had a hard two days of it, and now she felt Almighty God might well have pity on her, and leave her a week or even a fortnight of quiet, until she pulled her little home together again. Jumbo ate placidly and contentedly; she knew by this his drinking bout was almost over. At last he pulled his cap well down over his eyes and lay back with his wide red face to the sun. She watched him, her hands up on her lap. He looked for all the world like a huge, fat, sulky child. He lay like that without stirring for some time; then he stretched out his legs, and rolled over and over and over downhill through the grass. He grunted with pleasure, and sat up blinking drowsily at her from the edge of the cinder path. She put her hand in her pocket. "Jim, will I give you the price of an ounce of 'baccy?" He stared up at her for a moment. "There did ne'er a letter come for me?" he asked, and her heart sank. "No, Jim," she said feebly, "what letter was it you were expecting?" "Never mind, you. Here, give us a couple of lob for a wet!" She counted him out six coppers and he stood up to go.

All the evening she worried herself about Pa Kenefick and his friends — though to be sure they were good-natured friendly boys. She was glad when Jumbo came in at tea-time; the great bulk of him stretched out in the corner gave her a feeling of security. He was almost in good humour again, and talked a little, telling her to shut up when her tongue wagged too much, or sourly abusing the "bummers" who had soaked him the evening before. She had cleared away the supper things when a motor-car drove up the road and stopped at the end of Melancholy Lane. Her heart misgave her. She ran to the door and looked out; there were two men coming up the lane, one of them wearing a mask; when they saw her they broke into a trot. "Merciful Jesus!" she screamed, and rushed in, banging and bolting the door behind her. Jumbo stood up slowly. "What is it?" he asked. "That letter." "What letter?" "I showed it to Pa Kenefick, that letter from the barrack." The blue veins rose on Jumbo's forehead as though they would burst. He could barely speak but rushed to the fireplace and swept the poker over her head. "If it's the last thing I ever do I'll have your sacred life!" he said in a hoarse whisper. "Let me alone! Let me alone!" she shrieked. "They're at the door!" She leaned her back against the door, and felt against her spine the lurch of a man's shoulder. Jumbo heard it; he watched her with narrowed, despairing eyes, and then beckoned her towards the back door. She went on before him on tiptoe and opened the door quietly for him. "Quick," he said, "name of Jasus, lift me up this." This was the back wall, which was fully twice his own height but had footholes by which he could clamber up. She held his feet in them, and puffing and growling, he scrambled painfully up, inch by inch, until his head was almost level with the top of the wall; then with a gigantic effort he slowly raised his huge body and laid it flat upon the spiny top. "Keep them back, you!" he said. "Here," she called softly up to him, "take this," and he bent down and caught the poker.

It was dark in the little kitchen. She crept to the door

and listened, holding her breath. There was no sound. She was consumed with anxiety and impatience. Suddenly little Johnny sat up and began to howl. She grasped the key and turned it in the lock once; there was no sound; at last she opened the door slowly. There was no one to be seen in the lane. Night was setting in — maybe he would dodge them yet. She locked the screaming child in behind her and hurried down to the archway.

The motor-car was standing where it had stopped and a man was leaning over the wheel smoking a cigarette. He looked up and smiled at her. "Didn't they get him yet?" he asked, "No," she said mechanically. "Ah cripes!" he swore, "with the help of God they'll give him an awful end when they ketch him." She stood there looking up and down the road in the terrible stillness: there were lamps lighting behind every window but not a soul appeared. At last a strange young man in a trench-coat rushed down the lane towards them. "Watch out there," he cried. He's after giving us the slip. Guard this lane and the one below, don't shoot unless you can get him." He doubled down the road and up the next laneway.

The young man in the car topped his cigarette carefully, put the butt end in his waistcoat pocket and crossed to the other side of the road. He leaned nonchalantly against the wall and drew a heavy revolver. She crossed too and stood beside him. An old lamplighter came up one of the lanes from the city and went past them to the next gas-lamp, his torch upon his shoulder. "He's a brute of a man," the driver said consolingly, "sure, I couldn't but hit him in the dark itself. But it's a shame now they wouldn't have a gas-lamp at that end of the lane, huh!" The old lamplighter disappeared up the road, leaving two or three pale specks of light behind him.

They stood looking at the laneways each end of a little row of cottages, not speaking a word. Suddenly the young man drew himself up stiffly against the wall and raised his left hand towards the fading sky. "See that?" he said gleefully. Beyond the row of cottages a figure rose slowly

36

against a chimney-pot; they could barely see it in the twilight, but she could not doubt who it was. The man spat upon the barrel of his gun and raised it upon his crooked elbow; then the dark figure leaped out as it were upon the air and disappeared among the shadows of the houses. "Jasus!" the young man swore softly, "wasn't that a great pity?" She came to her senses in a flash. "Jumbo!" she shrieked, "me poor Jumbo! He's kilt, he's kilt!" and began to weep and clap her hands. The man looked at her in comical bewilderment. "Well, well!" he said, "to think of that! And are you his widda, ma'am?" "God melt and wither you!" she screamed and rushed away towards the spot where Jumbo's figure had disappeared.

At the top of the lane a young man with a revolver drove her back. "Is he kilt?" she cried. "Too well you know he's not kilt," the young man replied savagely. Another wearing a mask came out of a cottage and said "He's dished us again. Don't stir from this. I'm going round to Samson's Lane." "How did he manage it?" the first man asked. "Over the roofs. This place is a network, and the people won't stir a finger to help us."

For hours that duel in the darkness went on, silently, without a shot being fired. What mercy the people of the lanes showed to Jumbo was a mercy they had never denied to any hunted thing. His distracted wife went back to the road. Leaving the driver standing alone by his car she tramped up and down staring up every tiny laneway. It did not enter her head to run for assistance. On the opposite side of the road another network of lanes, all steep-sloping, like the others, or stepped in cobbles, went down into the heart of the city. These were Jumbo's only hope of escape, and that was why she watched there, glancing now and then at the maze of lights beneath her.

Ten o'clock rang out from Shandon — shivering, she counted the chimes. Then down one of the lanes from the north she heard a heavy clatter of ironshod feet. Clatter, clatter, clatter; the feet drew nearer, and she heard other, lighter, feet pattering swiftly behind. A dark figure emerged through the archway, running with frantic speed. She rushed out into the middle of the road to meet it, sweeping her shawl out on either side of her head like a dancer's sash. "Jumbo, me lovely Jumbo!" she screamed. "Out of me way, y'ould crow!" the wild quarry panted, flying past.

She heard him take the first flight of steps in the southern laneway at a bound. A young man dashed out of the archway a moment after and gave a hasty look around him. Then he ran towards her and she stepped out into the lane to block his passage. Without swerving he rushed into her at full speed, sweeping her off her feet, but she drew the wide black shawl about his head as they fell and rolled together down the narrow sloping passage. They were at the top of the steps and he still struggled frantically to free himself from the filthy enveloping shawl. They rolled from step to step, to the bottom, he throttling her and cursing furiously at her strength; she still holding the shawl tight about his head and shoulders. Then the others came and dragged him off, leaving her choking and writhing upon the ground.

But by this time Jumbo was well beyond their reach.

III

Next morning she walked dazedly about the town, stopping every policeman she met and asking for Jumbo. At the military barrack on the hill they told her she would find him in one of the city police barracks. She explained to the young English officer who spoke to her about Pa Kenefick, and how he could be captured, and for her pains was listened to in wide-eyed disgust. But what she could not understand in the young officer's attitude to her, Jumbo, sitting over the fire in the barrack day-room, had already been made to understand, and she was shocked to see him so pale, so sullen, so broken. And this while she was panting with pride at his escape! He did not even fly at her as she had feared he would, nor indeed abuse her at all. He merely looked up and said with the bitterness of utter resignation, "There's the one that brought me down!" An old soldier, he was cut to the heart that the military would not take him in, but had handed him over to the police for protection. "I'm no use to them now," he said, "and there's me thanks for all I done. They'd as soon see me out of the way; they'd as soon see the poor old crature that served them out of the way." "It was all Pa Kenefick's doings," his wife put in frantically, "it was no one else done it. Not that my poor slob of a man ever did him or his any harm. . . ." At this the policemen round her chuckled and Jumbo angrily bade her be silent. "But I told the officer of the swaddies where he was to be found," she went on unheeding. "What was that?" the policemen asked eagerly, and she told them of how she had found Pa Kenefick in the little cottage up the hill.

Every day she went to see Jumbo. When the weather was fine they sat in the little garden behind the barrack, for it was only at dusk that Jumbo could venture out and then only with military or police patrols. There were very few on the road who would speak to her now, for on the night after Jumbo's escape the little cottage where Pa Kenefick had stayed had been raided and smashed up by masked policemen. Of course, Pa and his friends were gone. She hated the neighbours, and dug into her mind with the fear of what might happen to Jumbo was the desire to be quit of Pa Kenefick. Only then, she felt in her blind headlong way, would Jumbo be safe. And what divil's notion took her to show him the letter? She'd swing for Pa, she said, sizing up to the policemen.

And Jumbo grew worse and worse. His face had turned from brick-red to grey. He complained always of pain and spent whole days in bed. She had heard that there was a cure for his illness in red flannel, and had made him a nightshirt of red flannel in which he looked more than ever like a ghost, his hair grey, his face quite colourless, his fat paws growing skinny under the wide crimson sleeves.

He applied for admission to the military hospital, which was within the area protected by the troops, and the request was met with a curt refusal. That broke his courage. To the military for whom he had risked his life he was only an informer, a common informer, to be left to the mercy of their enemy when his services were no longer of value. The policemen sympathised with him, for they too were despised by the "swaddies" as makers of trouble, but they could do nothing for him. And when he went out walking under cover of darkness with two policemen for an escort the people turned and laughed at him. He heard them, and returned to the barrack consumed with a rage that expressed itself in long fits of utter silence or sudden murderous outbursts.

She came in one summer evening when the fit was on him, to find him struggling in the dayroom with three of the policemen. They were trying to wrest a loaded carbine from his hands. He wanted blood, he shouted, blood, and by Christ they wouldn't stop him. They wouldn't, they wouldn't, he repeated, sending one of them flying against the hearth. He'd finish a few of the devils that were twitting him before he was plugged himself. He'd shoot everyone, man, woman, and child that came in his way. His frenzy was terrifying and the three policemen were swung this way and that, to right and left, as the struggle swept from wall to door and back. Then suddenly he collapsed and lay unconscious upon the floor. When they brought him round with whiskey he looked from one to the other, and drearily, with terrible anguish, he cursed all the powers about him, God, the King, the republicans, Ireland, and the country he had served.

"Kimberley, Pietermaritzburg, Bethlem, Bloemfontein," he moaned. "Ah, you thing, many's the hard day I put down for you! Devil's cure to me for a crazy man! Devil's cure to me, I say! With me cane and me busby and me scarlet coat — 'twas aisy you beguiled me! . . . The curse of God on you! . . . Tell them to pay me passage, d'you hear me? Tell them to pay me passage, and I'll go out to Inja and fight the blacks for you!"

It was easy to see whom he was talking to.

"Go the road resigned, Jim," his wife counselled timidly from above his head. Seeing him like this she could already believe him dying.

"I will not. . . . I will not go the road resigned."

". . . to His blessed and holy Will," she babbled.

Lifting his two fists from the ground he thumped upon his chest like a drum.

"'Tisn't sickness that ails me, but a broken heart," he cried. "Tell them to pay me passage! Ah, why didn't I stay with the lovely men we buried there, not to end my days as a public show. . . . They put the croolety of the world from them young, the creatures, they put the croolety of the world from them young!"

The soldiers had again refused to admit him to the military hospital. Now the police had grown tired of him, and on their faces he saw relief, relief that they would soon be shut of him, when he entered some hospital in the city, where everyone would know him, and sooner or later his enemies would reach him. He no longer left the barrack. Disease had changed that face of his already; the only hope left to him now was to change it still further. He grew a beard.

And all this time his wife lay in wait for Pa Kenefick. Long hours on end she watched for him over her half-door. Twice she saw him pass by the laneway, and each time snatched her shawl and rushed down to the barrack, but by the time a car of plain-clothes men drove up to the Kenefick's door Pa was gone. Then he ceased to come home at all, and she watched the movements of his sister and mother. She even trained little Johnny to follow them, but the child was too young and too easily outdistanced. When she came down the road in the direction of the city, all the women standing at their doors would walk in and shut them in her face.

One day the policeman on duty at the barrack door told her gruffly that Jumbo was gone. He was in hospital somewhere; she would be told where if he was in any danger. And she knew by the tone in which he said it that the soldiers had not taken Jumbo in; that somewhere he was at the mercy of his changed appearance and assumed name, unless, as was likely, he was already too far gone to make it worth the "rebels" while to shoot him. Now that she could no longer see him there was a great emptiness in her life, an emptiness that she filled only with brooding and hatred. Everything within her had turned to bitterness against Pa Kenefick, the boy who had been the cause of it all, to whom she had foolishly shown the letter and who had brought the "dirty Shinners" down on her, who alone had cause to strike at Jumbo now that he was a sick and helpless man.

"God, give me strength!" she prayed. "I'll sober him. O God, I'll put him in a quiet habitation!"

She worked mechanically about the house. A neighbour's averted face or the closing of a door in her path brought her to such a pitch of fury that she swept out into the road, her shawl stretched out behind her head, and tore up and down, screaming like a madwoman; sometimes leaping into the air with an obscene gesture; sometimes kneeling in the roadway and cursing those that had affronted her; sometimes tapping out a few dance steps, a skip to right and a skip to left, just to rouse herself. "I'm a bird alone!" she shrieked, "a bird alone and the hawks about me! Good man, clever man, handsome man, I'm a bird alone!" And "That they might rot and wither, root and branch, son and daughter, born and unborn; that every plague and pestilence might end them and theirs; that they might be called in their sins" – this was what she prayed in the traditional formula, and the neighbours closed their doors softly and crossed themselves. For a week or more she was like a woman possessed.

IV

Then one day when she was standing by the archway

she saw Pa Kenefick and another man come down the road. She stood back without being seen, and waited until they had gone by before she emerged and followed them. It was no easy thing to do upon the long open street that led to the quays, but she pulled her shawl well down over her eyes, and drew up her shoulders so that at a distance she might look like an old woman. She r eached the foot of the hill without being observed, and after that, to follow them through the crowded, narrow sidestreets of the city where every second woman wore a shawl was comparatively easy. But they walked so fast it was hard to keep up with them, and several times she had to take short-cuts that they did not know of, thus losing sight of them for the time being. Already they had crossed the bridge, and she was growing mystified; this was unfamiliar country and, besides, the pace was beginning to tell on her. They had been walking now for a good two miles and she knew that they would soon outdistance her. And all the time she had seen neither policeman nor soldier.

Gasping she stood and leaned against a wall, drawing the shawl down about her shoulders for a breath of air. "Tell me, ma'am," she asked of a passer-by, "where do this road go to?" "This is the Mallow Road, ma'am," the other said, and since Jumbo's wife made no reply she asked was it any place she wanted. "No indeed," Jumbo's wife answered without conviction. The other lowered her voice and asked sympathetically, "Is it the hospital you're looking for, poor woman?" Jumbo's wife stood for a moment until the question sank in. "The hospital?" she whispered. "The hospital? Merciful God Almighty!" Then she came to her senses. "Stop them!" she screamed, rushing out into the roadway, "stop them!" Murder! Murder! Stop them!"

The two men who by this time were far ahead heard the shout and looked back. Then one of them stepped out into the middle of the road and signalled to a passing car. They leaped in and the car drove off. A little crowd had gathered upon the path, but when they understood what the woman's screams signified they melted silently away.

Only the woman to whom she had first spoken remained. "Come with me, ma'am," she said. "'Tis only as you might say a step from this."

A tram left them at the hospital gate and Jumbo's wife and the other woman rushed in. She asked for Jumbo Geany, but the porter looked at her blankly and asked what ward she was looking for. "There were two men here a minute ago," she said frantically, "where are they gone to?" "Ah," he said "now I have you! They're gone over to St. George's Ward. . . ."

In St. George's Ward at that moment two or three nuns and a nurse surrounded the house doctor, a tall young man who was saying excitedly, "I couldn't stop them, couldn't stop them! I told them he was at his last gasp, but they wouldn't believe me!" "He was lying there," said the nurse pointing to an empty bed, "when that woman came in with the basket, a sort of dealing woman she was. When she saw him she looked hard at him and then went across and drew back the bedclothes. "Is it yourself is there, Jumbo?" says she, and, poor man, he starts up in bed and says out loud-like "You won't give me away? Promise me you won't give me away." So she laughs and says, "A pity you didn't think of that when you gave Mike Kenefick the gun, Jumbo!" After she went away he wanted to get up and go home. I seen by his looks he was dying and I sent for the priest and Doctor Connolly, and he got wake-like, and that pair came in, asking for a stretcher, and ———" The nurse began to bawl.

Just then Jumbo's wife appeared, a distracted, terrified figure, the shawl drawn back from her brows, the hair falling about her face. "Jumbo Geany?" she asked. "You're too late," said the young doctor harshly, "they've taken him away." "No, come back, come back!" he shouted as she rushed towards the window that opened on to the garden at the back of the hospital, "you can't go out there!" But she wriggled from his grasp, leaving her old black shawl in his hands. Alone she ran across the little garden, to where another building jutted out and obscured the view of the walls. As she did so three shots rang out in rapid succession. She heard a gate slam; it was the little wicket gate on to another road; beside it was a stretcher with a man's body lying on it. She flung herself screaming upon the body, not heeding the little streams of blood that flowed from beneath the armpit and the head. It was Jumbo, clad only in a nightshirt and bearded beyond recognition. His long, skinny legs were naked, and his toes had not ceased to twitch. For each of the three shots there was a tiny wound, two over the heart and one in the temple, and pinned to the cheap flannelette nightshirt was a little typed slip that read

SPY.

They had squared her account with Jumbo at last.

Nightpiece with Figures

Preluded by one short squeak of its hinges, a door opens slowly and quietly into a dark and empty barn.

Framed in the doorway is the glow of an autumn night, figured with a faint tracery of starlight. It is evident that the barn is pitched high above some valley because nothing obscures the lower portion of the doorway but the shadow of heaped straw. At last, and only after a whispered conversation outside, the upper portion too is filled, this time by a man's figure seen in dim silhouette. He stumbles headlong into the barn, his feet catching in and rustling the dry straw; and now the bright oblong becomes the setting for a shadow show in which a second, third, and fourth figure take part. Somewhere very near a cow moos, and hooves clatter with a light thud. The first man tripping in the darkness utters an oath, and flings himself wearily on to a heap of straw in one corner. The whispered conversation outside continues, but more animatedly; then a light flares up and the face of a young man, dark, sardonic, and reckless is seen, bent for a moment above the rosy vessel of his cupped hands. He smokes, shading the glow of the cigarette as he does so.

"What is it, Peter?" the first man whispers from his corner.

"Nothing, nothing. Do you want to smoke?"

"Not now – why?"

"We mustn't smoke inside because of the straw."

"Oh, is that all!"

A second man comes and sits beside the first, and they converse under their breath with subdued chuckles. Still another voice is heard outside, also in a whisper, but gradually rising as the speaker gives rein to his excitement.

"Believe you me, comrade, that man have us all taped. Twiced I seen him outside the gate here after dark and never was there rhyme nor raison for his presence. I said nothing but I thought the more. Then I got the first threatening letter I was telling you about signed 'Black Hand Gang' in red ink – pretending it was blood! – and three days later comes another signed 'I.R.A.' Mind you, I had no proof it was himself that wrote them, but I followed my natural reasonings and seduced the fact. 'So-ho! my esteemed friend,' says I, 'this is how *you* carry on. But I have no cause to be afraid of the Irish Republican Army. . . .'" So I sent him a threatening letter signed 'O.C.' letting him know pretty plain that he was being watched too, and since that day he never darkened this gate of ours . . . never! Now that's strange, isn't it, comrade?"

"Yes," yawns the man who is smoking, "ye-e-e-s, that's strange. Good God, how tired I am!"

"Naturally, naturally. So what I say is: You send him a letter on printed paper, paper with I.R.A. printed on the top and see what effect that will have. Say 'You are being closely observed,' or words to that effect; 'a trusty friend of ours has constantly noted your movements and reported them to the proper quarter.' You see, I've thought it out, and if you leave me wan sheet of official paper I'll guarantee to give him many a sleepless night."

They were interrupted by the sound of heavy footsteps. The young men sit up and listen tensely, but the one who has been speaking reassures them with a backward wave of his hand. Meanwhile, the slow footsteps come nearer; they are the noisy clatter of loose footwear. The young man Peter, who has been smoking, tops the cigarette between his fingers and stands inside the door. A faint yellow light begins to stream around the doorway, and as it is swung backward and forward it projects a gradually widening circle of visibility over the loose cobbles among which the rain is still lodged from yesterday; while, with each jolt given to the lantern, the young men hear a loud, rhythmical sigh, a sigh that expresses habit rather than necessity. Then a figure stands framed in the doorway, carrying in one hand a lighted lantern and in the other a basket. The young man who is standing there, takes off his hat and says politely, "Good night, Sister," and the two men in the corner bend forward until their faces are revealed by the lantern, smiling and respectful, and do likewise.

The nun — for it is a nun — is dressed all in white. She is an old woman with bright, crust-like, apple-red cheeks, and her skirts are now drawn up about her knees. Everything she does is done slowly, with the pronounced emphasis of old age, as at this moment when she stands looking in, the lantern held a foot or less before her, her little blue eyes screwed up, each inside a score of wrinkles, and her breath coming in dry, wheezy, asthmatic pants.

"*Dia bhur mbeatha, a dhaoine maithe,*" she says after a moment and the Gaelic salutation that means "God be your life" is followed by a quaint gust of antique mirth.

Still chuckling she lays down her basket inside the door, raises herself slowly with yet another sigh and turns to the man who has been speaking.

"Two of the loveliest calves you ever seen, Dan," she says. "Two little jewels, praise be to you, God! So now that old caubogue, Jer Callaghan, won't be putting the milk of the cow we bought from him on the Department sheet."

"I was telling our young frinds what a grand farm we had here, Sister," he says.

"Tch! Tch! Tch! . . . Nothing for fifty miles around to equal it. Nothing. . . ."

She looks at the young men, and in the half-light which the lantern casts up on her round, red, toothless, laughing face there is an extravagance of pride and joy. Her voice as she continues startles them by its masculine resonance.

"I don't know what they'll do without me at all at all

when the Lord God calls me home! I don't indeed know what they'll do without me. I say to Reverend Mother when she comes round to Galilee – that's what we calls our end of the building, Galilee – I say to her, 'Ach, wait till I'm growing purty daisies in the ploteen beyond, and you'll see how fond of me ye were – then you'll see!' "

She is chuckling again, but continues in a lower tone and more tenderly.

"Ach, sure, I do be only taking a rise out of her, boys. They're all fond of me though I speaks saucy enough to them at times, the creatures – that's when things go agin me. But then we must be saying something, hey?"

"We're all fond of you, Sister," Dan the farm labourer says unctuously, and then dodges out of the way of her hand which she raises at him in mock indignation.

"Ach, go 'way, y'ould hypocrite and you're nothing else!" She turns on the young men once more, pointing a bony forefinger at the basket. "There's bread and mate for ye there, boys, and if ye want anything else ye've only to ask for it. And ye've my prayers as well, so that's mate for body and soul. . . . Ye night-walking blackguards!"

She is off again into her deep, merry, asthmatic chuckle. As it subsides into a prolonged fit of coughing she raises the lantern to the handsome reckless face of the young man standing beside the door. He is clearly the leader of the trio.

"What's your name?"

"Peter Mulcahy, Sister."

"There's none of ye there I know?"

"No, Sister."

"None of ye was here before?"

"No, Sister."

"I hope ye'll come again, God bless ye! I'm Sister Alophonsus, and though I likes me little joke I'm a good-natured old woman, so I am. And I've a great *gradh* for anyone that lifts his hand for Holy Ireland. My father was a friend of Bryan Dillon. Did you ever hear tell of Bryan Dillon, young man?"

"I did, Sister. He was the Fenian."

"So he was, the Fenian, Brienie Dill we called him. My father — the Heavens be his bed — was a great friend of his. Many's the night they talked powder and shot until the break of day. Brienie Dill was a little hunchback, but the neatest little hunchback you ever seen. I remember well the day he was left out of gaol, though I was only a slip of a girl then. There was stones flying that day in the Barrack Sthream I can tell you. . . . And my father was one of the men that buried the pikes in the Quakers' graveyard. Did you know there was pikes buried there, young man?"

"No, Sister."

"There was then. Pikes buried in the Quakers' graveyard. And 'God send,' says Brienie Dill, 'God in Heaven send they rise before the Quakers do!' "

They all laugh at this. She laughs with them, and shaken by her gusty mirth the lantern rocks to right and left in her hand. Suddenly the men start at the sound of light, quick footsteps, followed immediately by the rustling of a dress against the wall of the barn. In a moment a second woman's figure is upon them. The light just catches the dainty forehead and the rim of starched cloth beneath her veil. The old nun, who has heard nothing, has just raised her apron to her eyes to wipe away the slow tears of laughter that fill them when her arm is caught from behind by the newcomer.

"Don't be afraid, Sister!" a young voice whispers good-humouredly. "It's only me."

There is something grotesque about the way in which Sister Alphonsus proceeds to assure herself of the young nun's identity. She lifts the lantern until it is shining full into the other's face, and before the young nun in laughing protest has forced it aside, the men have received a picture of her that impresses itself forever on their memories. Unlike the farm sister she is dressed in black, and is obviously a choir nun. Her face is unusually broad at the jaw, but this instead of making her features appear harsh makes them appear curiously tender. Her face is almost colourless, her nose short; her eyes are jet black under long black lashes that give them a dreamy look; but over all her features is a strange expression which is not at all dreamy or tender, but anxious, abrupt and painfully, sensitively, wide awake. Yet she is very girlish, slim and sprightly; and her appearance as she stands in the doorway suggests to the three hunted men a visionary, enchanted youth, that wakes a sort of pang within them, a pang of desire and loss. She is carrying some rugs on her arm and hands them to the other nun; then with one hand on the jamb of the door in an attitude that more than suggests flight, she looks in.

"I must rush back, Sister," she whispers hastily. "Good night, boys, and God bless you!"

"Good night, Sister" they reply, and Dan, standing in the background hat in hand, chimes in with a respectful "Good night."

"Nobody there that I know?" she asks, delaying, her dark eyes puckered up in an attempt to pierce the shadows. "You are all from the city?"

"Yes, Sister."

"How have the city fellows gone? What about Dan Lahy? Jo Godwin?"

"Free State Army."

"And Denny, Michael Denny?"

"The same."

"God forgive them! Anyone else of that crowd gone over?"

"All but two."

"They used to stay out here in the old days – you knew that?"

"Have you heard about Sean Clery?"

A sudden bitterness has crept into the voice that speaks from the corner of the barn, a bitterness that communicates itself immediately to the other men, and dramatises the instant in their minds as well as in the mind of the young nun, so that her reply when it comes brims the cup of emotion for all.

"My sister told me. Poor Sean – God have mercy on

him!"

"God save us from our own!" the bitter voice corrects her quietly. "Taken out the road and shot to pieces like a mad dog! Did you know him, Sister?"

"A little – oh, yes I did; of course I knew him when he was a boy. . . . They gave him a dreadful end. . . ."

"It's a cruel, cruel thing, this fighting!" the old nun puts in loudly and vehemently. "A cruel, silly thing! They must be wicked men to do a deed like that. Ah, if they were here now Sister Alophonsus would give them a bit of her mind, so she would!"

"Be quiet, Sister!" the other says fearfully. "You talk too loud you know."

Sister Alphonsus sighs.

"Ach, sure they don't mind how loud I talk. They hears me talking always to the cows."

"And do you talk to the cows, Sister?" the young man called Peter asks, as though to change the conversation.

"Of course I do talk to them. Cows are foolish beasts – they're foolisher than pigs, cows are, and you'd get no good of them at all if you didn't talk sensibly to them and tell them what you want."

There is a heavy silence broken only by the stirring of beasts in a nearby byre, and something in the silence suggests that the young nun is suffering deeply. After a little she breaks the stillness that has already grown too oppressive for all but the old woman immersed in her angry maternal dreams.

"And the people?"

"Indifferent," says Peter hardily.

"Against us," says the bitter voice from the darkness.

"Just as it is with us here. In the old days we were all united – we knew that the boys were sleeping in the outhouses; we sent them out food and medals and scapulars; before we went to bed each night we said a prayer for them. Now there's no one left to pray for you but old Sister Alphonsus and myself."

"No one, no one!" chimes in Sister Alphonsus. " 'Tis

true for you, alanna, they all reneged. But Sister Alophonsus, the ould Fenian, didn't renege. She's as true to her counthry now as ever she was."

"If you were out with us for a day or two you'd see it all," the voice from the darkness continues. "Where is the sovereign Irish people we used to hear so much about a year or two ago? Sorry, Sister, we haven't any heroes left, but we can always find you a few informers." A revolver clacks open in the darkness and the voice continues half-humourously, "Holy Ireland! Holy Ireland, how are you?"

"Oh, chuck it! Chuck it for Heaven's sake!" the young man called Peter says irritably.

"*Och, a Dhe! Och, a Dhe!*" Sister Alphonsus sighs, turning away.

"Oh, informers, hadn't we always our share of them?" the young nun asks quickly. "But never mind what happens to us, never mind the people, never mind the informers! Ireland will outlive them all."

There is a sudden throb of male passion in the voice, a sudden bursting out of emotions that have been too long suppressed.

"Ireland?" the young man in the corner asks cynically.

"Yes. Ireland. We haven't been the first and we won't be the last."

Dan, the old farmhand, weary of the conversation that goes on so far above his head, moves away on tiptoe over the cobbles, downhill, and watching his retreating figure sink down against the autumnal sky she shivers slightly.

"What are your names?" she asks suddenly, and her voice has lost its overtone of passion. The three men tell her their names shyly, one after another.

"Michael . . . Peter . . . Liam," she repeats letting each name sink into her memory. "I'll remember your names, and pray that you'll come safely out of it all — and be happy," she adds as an afterthought. "And you'll pray for me, won't you? Sister Josephine is my name."

"And Sister Alophonsus! Don't forget old Sister

Alophonsus!" the old woman says warningly.

"Good night, boys."

"Good night, Sister."

"Good night, Peter," she says with a quick, dainty movement of her head to the young man standing by the door; a gesture that seems unerringly to separate him from the others and predict for him some experience richer than theirs — then, as silently and swiftly as she had come, the young nun goes.

Sister Alphonsus, sighing with the same antique vehemence, hangs the lantern on a hook from the low roof of the barn.

"The light of Heaven to our souls on the last day!" she mumbles earnestly. . . . There's your rugs. . . . The child is supposed to be nursing old Mother Agatha. She must have slipped out when she was asleep and got the rugs on the sly. . . . Hot blood! Hot Blood! . . . She's not happy. . . . She's too hasty. I tell her not to take things to heart so, but she do, she do! Hot Blood! . . . Why should she mind what they say to her? I've put up with them now these forty year. Forty years on the fifteenth of February, boys, if the good God lets me live to see the day."

Sighing still she bids them good night in her soft West Munster Gaelic and goes, latching the door noisily behind her. The lantern barely illumines the little barn and the three figures stretched upon the straw. They eat, exchanging an occasional word that does not express at all what is in their minds. Then Peter quenches the lamp and everything is dark and silent but for the stirring of beasts in a nearby byre. But neither the silence, nor the fragrance of the straw on which they lie, nor the food they have taken brings sleep to them — not for a long time.

They are all happy as though some wonderful thing had happened to them, but what the wonderful thing is they could not say, and with their happiness is mixed a melancholy as strange and perturbing, as though life itself and all the modes of life were inadequate. It is not a bitter melancholy like the melancholy of defeat, and in the morning, when they take to the country roads again, it will have passed.

But the memory of the young nun will not pass so lightly from their minds.

September Dawn

I

It was late September of the finest autumn that had been known for years. For five crowded days the column had held out, flying from one position to another, beaten about by a dozen companies of regular soldiers. At Glenmanus they had taken shelter among the trees, and fought for a few hours with the river protecting them, but, a second column of soldiers having crossed by a temporary bridge a mile or two up the road, they had found themselves completely outflanked. Then they had fought their way across country; seven men holding one ditch while the other seven retreated to the next. Again they had been headed off and again had changed direction. "It was a sort of game a schoolboy would play with a beetle," remarked Keown.

This time they had been trapped by a column coming from the direction of Mallow. Finally, in desperation, they had come back by night and along a different route to their old stronghold in Glenmanus, and here they rested while Keown and Hickey, standing apart, held counsel.

Hickey, dressed in a black coat and green riding-breeches, was very tall and slim. He had the reputation of being as conscientious as he was inhuman, and there was a strain of fanaticism in his pale face and in the steely eyes behind their large horn-rimmed spectacles. It was the face of a young scientist or a young priest. He lacked imagination, people said. He also lacked humour. But he was a good soldier and cautious where men's lives were concerned. His companion was stocky and pugnacious, with a fat, good-humoured face and a left eye that squinted atrociously. He was unscrupulous, good-natured, and unreliable, and had a bad reputation for his ways with women. He even boasted of it, and added, with a wink of his sound eye, that there wasn't a parish in Munster where he couldn't find a home and children. He read much more than Hickey, and rarely went anywhere without a book in his pocket. It was most often an indecent French novel, but sometimes he carried about a book of verse which he read aloud to Hickey in his broad, bantering, countryman's voice. He liked to hear himself speak, and, when his column was in billet, practised elocution before a mirror. The two men now stood on the river bank. Hickey idly disturbing the sluggish water with a switch, and Keown, small and ungainly, with a rifle swung across his right shoulder and a sandwich in his hand, eyeing him in silence.

After about ten minutes they returned. Hickey glanced coldly at the twelve volunteers sitting on the grass, chewing sandwiches and drinking spring water out of a rusty water-bottle. Their rifles lay beside them. Most of them had doffed their hats and caps. An autumn sun shone warmly and brightly overhead, and cast spotlights through the yellowing leaves upon their flushed young faces, upturned to his, and their bare brown throats.

"We have decided to disband the column, men," he said briefly.

"Disband? Do you mean we are to go home?" one of them asked with a quick look of dismay.

"Yes, there's nothing else for it. It's disband or go down together; we can't carry on as we've been doing."

They stared blankly at him.

"And the rifles, the equipment? What are we to do with them?"

"Dump them."

"Dump them — after five days?"

"You heard what I said."

"We're genuinely sorry, boys," Keown put in kindly.

"Jim and I appreciate more than we can say the way you've stuck by us through it all. Don't think we're ungrateful. We aren't. We've made friends amongst you that we'll always be proud of. But it's better we should lose you this way than another. We want to live for Ireland, not to die for it, and die we will if we stick together any longer. There's no use blinking that. The country here is too damn flat, too damn thickly populated, and there are too many roads."

There was silence for a moment. The men sat looking desperately at one another and at their leaders. Suddenly one of them, a farm labourer with a thick red moustache, who had been tying up a packet of sandwiches tossed it away; it broke through the leaves, and fell with a little splash in the river. He rose and threw aside his cloth bandolier, and then began to unbuckle his khaki belt. His face was pale, and his hands fumbled nervously at the catch. The others rose too, one after another.

"'Faith, it'll be a comfort to sleep at home after a week of this, neighbours."

The speaker was a handsome youth, scarcely more than a boy.

"Ah, my lad," said the other man bitterly, "you'll sleep in a different bed, and a harder bed, before this week is out, and serve you right."

The speech was greeted with a murmur of approval.

"We must only risk that," said Keown hastily. "After all you've only been away from home for a week; they can't have spotted you so easily."

"Spotted us?" exclaimed the other angrily, squaring up to him. "Who talks about spotting? Or do you know who you're speaking to? Him and me came up all the way to fight at Passage. We're out of the one house, and we went off together in the dead of night on our bikes to join the brigade. We followed it to Macroom and we were sent back from that. Just as you're sending us back now. We're no seven-day soldiers, but, let me tell you, it's the last time I'll make a fool of myself for ye."

Keown shrugged his shoulders helplessly without replying.

It was the youngster who showed them where the old dump was. It was dug into the low wall that surrounded the wood, and after some difficulty they succeeded in locating it. He and Keown together took out the heavy stones, one by one, and revealed a deep hollow beneath the wall. There was a long box like a coffin in it, and half a dozen sheets of oilcloth, with some old greasy rags and a tin of oil. The rifles were gathered together – there was no time to oil them – and wrapped in the oilcloth. The same was done with bandoliers, belts, and bayonets. Only the two leaders kept their arms and equipment. Hickey did not even pretend to be interested in the funeral ceremony, but walked moodily about under the shadow of the trees, his spectacles glinting in the stray shafts of sunlight.

When the work was finished, the stones replaced, and all trace of fresh earth cleaned away, the twelve men, looking now merely what in ordinary life they were, farmers' sons or day-labourers, stood awkwardly about, hands behind their backs or buried in their trousers' pockets.

"And now, men, it's time we were going," said the youngster in a tone of authority; already he was testing his own leadership of the little group.

Keown grinned and held out his hand to the farm labourer who had spoken so rudely to him. It was taken in silence and held for a moment. The rough unsoldierly faces cleared, and a smile of tenderness, of companionship, crossed them. The youngster strode bravely over to Hickey's side, and held out his hand with all a boy's gaucherie.

"Well, good-bye, Mr. Hickey," he said jauntily. "See you soon again, I hope."

"Good-bye, Dermod, boy, and good luck," said Hickey, smiling faintly, as the others shambled over to say farewell.

Then with a last chorus of "Good luck" and "God be with you!" the little group dispersed among the trees, going in different directions to their own homes. Their voices grew faint in the distance and the two friends were left alone upon the river bank.

II

An hour later as they leaped across the fence above the wood a shot rang out and Keown's hat sailed along beside him to the ground. Hickey flattened himself against the ditch and raised his rifle, but Keown flung himself distractedly on the grass beside his hat, brushed it and contemplated regretfully the little hole on top.

"A man who'd do a thing like that," he commented with disgust, "would snatch a slice of bread out of an orphan's mouth!"

"But he's a good shot, Jim," he went on. "I will say that for him. He's a great shot. One, two, two and a half inches farther down and he'd have got me just where I wouldn't have known when. Ah, well! . . ." He picked himself up gingerly with head well bent. "A miss is as good as a mile, and talking of miles. . . ."

"I'll stay here until you get across the next field."

"And where do we go after that, Brother James?"

"It doesn't matter. Anywhere out of this; we can take our bearings later on."

"At this point in the battle General Hickey gave the order to retreat," murmured Keown, and scudded across the field, head low, his rifle trailing along the grass. Hickey looked down towards the road.

He could see nobody. The sun was high up in the centre of the heavens, and a great heat had come into the day. Beneath him was the wood, and the broad shallow river shone like steel through the reddening leaves. Beyond it the main road ran white and clear. Beyond the road another hill, more trees, and a house. The house one did not see from the wood, perched as it was like a bonnet on the brow of the hill, but from where he stood he had a clear view of it, outhouses and all. An old mansion of sorts it was, eighteenth century probably, with a wide carriage-way and steps up to the door. As he looked, the door opened and a figure appeared, dressed in white; it was a girl whose attention had been attracted by the shot, perhaps also by the knowledge that a column of irregulars was in the vicinity. It amused him to think that he had only to lift his hat or handkerchief on the barrel of his rifle for her to hear more from the same source. Despite his natural caution, the idea became a temptation; he fingered with the safety-catch of his rifle, and began to calculate how many of the enemy there were. Scarcely more than a dozen, he thought, or they would have shown more daring in their approach to the wood. She shaded her eyes with her hand, searching the whole neighbourhood. To wave to her now would be good fun, but dangerous.

He looked round for Keown and saw him hurrying back. Clearly, there was something wrong. But Keown, seeing his attention attracted, came no farther, and made off in another direction, waving his hand in a way that showed the need for haste. Hickey followed, keeping all the time in shelter of the ditch.

When he reached the gap towards which Keown had run, he found him there, sitting on his hunkers, his tongue licking the corners of his mouth, his hands gripping nervously at his rifle.

"James," he said with affected coolness, "we must run for it. My tactics are particularly strong upon that point. Leave it to me, James! In the military college I was considered a dab at retreats."

He pointed to a field that sloped upward from where they crouched to the brow of the hill.

"I'm afraid we'll be exposed crossing the field, but we must only risk it. After that we'll have cover enough. Ready?"

"Are there many of them?" asked Hickey.

"As thick as snakes in the D.T.s. Are you ready?"

"Ready!" said Hickey.

He closed his eyes and ran. For a full half minute he heard nothing but the beating of his own heart and the soft thud their feet made upon the grass. The sunlight swam in a rosy mist before his darkened eyes, and it seemed as if at any moment the ground might rise out of this nowhere of rosy light and hit him. Suddenly a dozen rifles signalled their appearance with a burst of rapid firing, and immediately on top of this came the unmistakable staccato whirring of a machine-gun. His eyes started open with the shock, and he saw Keown, almost doubled in two, running furiously and well ahead of him. He put on speed. The machine-gun fire grew more intense until it was almost continuous. Then it stopped, and only the rifles kept up their irregular rattle until they too trailed off and were still. It was only then he realised that he was under cover, and that what was driving him forward at such speed was the impetus of his original fear.

Keown waited for him, leaning against an old white-thorn tree, his sides perceptibly widening and narrowing as he breathed. His head seemed to be giddy and shook slightly; his trembling hands mechanically sought in every pocket for cigarettes. A faint smile played about the corners of his mouth, and when he spoke his words came almost in a whisper.

"Rotten shooting, James, but still a narrow squeak."

"A very narrow squeak," said Hickey, and said no more, for his own head trembled as if a great hand were holding it in a tight grip and pushing it from side to side at a terrific speed. He stumbled along beside his companion without a word.

About a mile up the glen there was a stream. The two men knelt together beside it and plunged their faces deep into the gleaming, ice cold water. They rose, half-choking, but dipped into it again, their dripping forelocks blinding their eyes. When the water had cleared a little they sank their hands in, and, still in silence, drank from their cupped palms. Then they dried hands and faces with their handkerchiefs, and each lit a cigarette, taking long pulls of the invigorating smoke.

"It looks to me," said Keown, with a faint gleam of his old cheerfulness, "as if this was to be a busy day."

"It looks to me as if they wanted to locate the column," Hickey added wearily. "And now the column is broken up we'd be fools to hang round."

"You want to get back west?"

"I do."

"Home to our mountains."

"Precisely."

"I don't know how that's to be managed."

"I do. If once we get outside this accursed ring it will be simple enough. Probably it's closing in already. If we can hold out until nightfall we may be able to slip through; then we have only to cross by Mallow to Donoughmore, and after that everything will be plain sailing."

"It sounds good. Do you know the way?"

"No, but I think we might get a few miles north of this, don't you?"

"Out of range, Jim, out of range! That's the main thing, the first principle of tactics."

They shouldered their rifles and went on, keeping to the fields, and taking what cover they could. Hickey's legs were barely able to support him. Keown was in no better condition. Every now and then he sighed, and cast longing glances at the sun which was still upon the peak of heaven and let fall its vertical beams upon the wide expanse of open country, with its green meadow-lands and greying stubble, its golden furze, and squat, pink, all-too-neat farmhouses; or looked disconsolately at the chain of mountains that closed the farthest horizon with a delicate, faint line of blue.

"I know where my mother's son would like to be now," he said with facetious melancholy.

"So do I," said Hickey.

"In Kilnamartyr?" asked Keown, thinking still of the mountains. "God, Kilnamartyr and wan melodious night in Moran's!"

"No. Not in Kilnamartyr. At home – in the city."

"Your paradise would never do for me, Jim. There are no women in it."

"Aren't there, now?"

"There are not, you old Mohammedan!"

"How do you know, Antichrist?"

"There aren't, there aren't, there aren't! I'd lay a hundred to one on that."

"You'd win."

"Of course I'd win! Don't I know your finicking, Jesuitical soul? You hate and fear women as you hate and fear the devil – and a bit more. It's a pity, Jim, it's a real pity, because, God increase you, you're a terror to fight; but there's as much poetry in your constitution as there is in a sardine-tin. Will you ever get married, Jim?"

"Not until we've won this war."

"And if we don't win it?"

"Oh, there's no if; we must win it!"

Keown cast an amused glance at his companion out of the corner of his eye, and they trudged on again in silence.

III

Five times that day they got the alarm and had to take to their heels. Three times it resulted in desultory fighting. One bout lasted a full three-quarters of an hour; it was hard, slogging, ditch-to-ditch fighting, with one holding back the enemy while the other got into position at the farther end of the field. The last alarm came while they were having tea in a farmer's house. There was no suspicion of treachery, and the soldiers, as unprepared as they, had walked up the boreen to the house for tea. The two friends left in haste by the back door, Keown hugging to his breast a floury half-cake snatched from the table in his hurry. The cake had cost him dear, because in securing it he had forgotten his hat (the hat which, as he assured Jim Hickey, he had earmarked as a present for one of his wives). They halved the hot cake and devoured it, regretting the fresh tea upon the table, and the mint of butter now being consumed by the soldiers.

But at last, drawing on to nightfall, they seemed to have left pursuit behind them and took their bearings. Hickey recognised the place. It was close to Mourneabbey and a few miles away lived an old aunt of his. He suggested sleeping there for the night, and Keown jumped at the idea, even consenting to put away his rifle and equipment until morning, lest their appearance should frighten the old woman.

It was darkening when they reached her house, and having stowed their rifles away in a dry wall, they made their way up the long winding boreen to the top of the hill. A sombre maternal peace enveloped the whole countryside; the fields were a rich green that merged into grey and farther off into a deep, shining purple. A stream flashed like a trail of white fire across the landscape. The beeches along the lane nodded down a withered leaf or two upon their heads, and the glossy trunks glowed a faint silver under the darkness of their boughs. A dog ran to meet them barking noisily.

The house was a long, low, whitewashed building with a four-sided roof, and outhouses on every side. The two men were greeted by Hickey's aunt, an old woman, doubled up with rheumatism, who beamed delightedly upon him through a pair of dark spectacles. They sat down to tea in the kitchen, a long whitewashed room with an open hearth, where the kettle swung from a chain over the fire. Everything in the house was simple and old-fashioned, the open hearth, the bellows one blows by turning a wheel, the churn, the two pictures that hung on opposite walls, one of Robert Emmet and the other of Parnell. Old-fashioned, but comfortable, with a peculiar warmth when she drew the shutters to and lit the lamp. And homely, when she pulled her chair up to the table and questioned Hickey about mother and sisters, tush-tushed playfully his being "on the run" (he said nothing of the rifles hidden in the wall or their experience during the day) and joked light-heartedly as old people will to whom realities are no longer such, but shadows that drift daily farther and farther away as their hold upon life slackens.

Parnell had been her last great love, and for her the hope of Irish independence had died with him. Hickey was moved by this strange isolation of hers, moved since now more than at any other time what had happened in those far-off days of elections, brass bands and cudgels seemed remote and insubstantial. And so they talked, each failing to understand the other.

Meanwhile, Keown kept one eye upon a young woman who moved silently about the kitchen as he took his meal. She was a country girl who helped the old lady with her housework. Her appearance had a peculiar distinction that was almost beauty. Very straight and slender she was with a broad face that tapered to a point at the chin, a curious unsmiling mouth, large, sensitive nostrils, and wide-set, melancholy eyes. Her hair was dull gold, and was looped up in a great heap at the poll. Her untidy clothes barely concealed a fine figure, and Keown watched with the appreciation of a connoisseur the easy motion of her body, so girlish yet so strong.

His attention was distracted from her by the appearance of a bottle of whiskey, and, ignoring Hickey's warning glance, he filled a stiff glass for himself and sipped it with unction. For a week past he had not been allowed to touch drink; this was one thing Hickey insisted on with fanatical zeal – no bad example must be given to the men.

When the two women had left the room to prepare a bed for their visitors, Keown said, leaning urgently across the table:

"Jim, I give you fair warning that I'm going to fall in love with that girl."

"You are not."

"I am, I tell you. And what's more she's going to fall in love with me, you old celebate! So I'm staying on. I've been virtuous too long. A whole week of it! My God, even the Crusaders——"

"You're drinking too much of that whiskey. Put it away!"

"Ah, shut up you, Father James! Aren't we on vacation, anyhow?"

When Hickey's aunt came back she led off the conversation again, but Hickey carefully watched his companion make free with the whiskey and cast bolder and bolder eyes at the girl, and, as he leaned across to fill himself a third glass, snatched the bottle away. That was enough, he said, forcing Keown off with one hand and with the other holding the bottle, and he remained deaf to Keown's assurances that he would take only a glass, a thimbleful, a drop, as he was tired and wanted to go to bed, as well as the old woman's pleading on his behalf that no doubt the young gentleman had had a tiring day and needed a little glass to cheer him up. Hickey could be obstinate when he chose, and he chose then; so Keown went off to bed, sticking out his tongue at him behind the old woman's back, and blinking angrily at the sleep that closed his eyelids in his own despite.

Hickey felt as if he too were more than half asleep, but he remained up until his aunt's husband returned from Mallow. He heard the pony and trap drive into the cobbled yard, and at last the old man entered, his lean brown face flushed with the cold air. The wind was rising, he said cheerfully, and sure enough it seemed to Hickey that he heard a first feeble rustle of branches about the house. "God sends winds to blow away the falling leaves," the old man said oracularly. "Time little Sheela was in bed," said his wife. The girl called Sheela smiled, and in her queer silent way disappeared into a little room off the kitchen. "That's another terrible rebel," the old woman went on, "though you wouldn't think it of her and the little she have to say. She was never a prouder girl than when she made the bed for the pair of ye tonight." " 'You never thought,' says I to her, 'I had such a fine handsome soldier nephew?' . . . Ah, God, ah, God, we weren't so wild in our young days!" "Happy days!" said her husband nodding and spitting into the ashes. "But not so wild," she repeated, "not so wild!" She brewed fresh tea, and then they sat into the fire and talked family history for what seemed to Hickey an intolerably long time. Once or twice he felt his head sag and realised that he had dropped off momentarily to sleep. It was his aunt who did most of the talking. Occasionally the old man collected his wits for some ponderous sentence, and having made the most of it nodded and smiled quietly with intense satisfaction. He had a brown, bony, innocent face and a short grey beard.

At last he rose and saying solemnly, "Even the foolish animal must sleep," went off to bed. Hickey followed him, leaving his aunt to quench the light. Even with Keown in it the house seemed spiritually still, abstracted, and lonely, and thinking of the danger of raids and arrests which their presence brought to it, he half-wished he had not come there. For worlds he would not have disturbed that old couple, spending their last days in childless, childish innocence, without much hope or fear.

He stood at the window of their room before striking a match. The room was a sort of lean-to above the servant's room downstairs, and smelt queerly of apples and decay. The window was low, very low, and he stood back from it. It gave but a faint light and outside he could distinguish nothing but the shadows of some trees grouped about the gable end. The wind, growing louder, pealed through them, and they creaked faintly, while the slightest of slight sounds, as of distant drumming, seemed to emanate from the boards and window-frame of the little bedroom. As he lit the candle and began to undress Keown stirred in the bed, and, raising his fat, pugnacious face and squint eye out of a tumble of white linen and dark hair, said thickly but with sombre indignation, "In spite of you I'll have that girl. Yes, my f-f-friend, in – spite – of you——!"

"Ah, go to sleep like a good man!" said Hickey crossly, and clad only in a light summer singlet, slipped into bed beside him.

IV

The wind! That was it, the wind! He could not have slept for long before it woke him. It blew with a sort of clumsy precision, rising slowly in great crescendos that shook the windowpanes and seemed to reverberate through the whole ramshackle house. The window was bright so there was no rain. "God sends winds to blow away the falling leaves," he thought with a smile.

He lay back and watched the window that seemed to grow brighter as he looked at it, and suddenly it became clear to him that his life was a melancholy, aimless life, and that all this endless struggle and concealment was but so much out of an existence that would mean little anyhow. He had left college two years before when the police first began hunting for him, and he doubted now whether it would ever be in his power to return. He was a different man, and most of the ties he had broken then he would never be able to resume. If they won, of course, the army would be open to him, but the army he knew would not content him long, for soldiering at best was only servitude, and he had lived too desperately to endure the hollow routine of barrack life. Besides, he was a scientist, not a soldier. And if they lost? (He thought bitterly of what Keown had suggested that afternoon and his own reply.) Of course, they mustn't lose, but suppose they did? What was there for him then? America? That was all – America! And his mother, who had worked so hard to educate him and had hoped so much of him, his mother would die, having seen him accomplish nothing, and he would be somewhere very far away. What use would anything be then? And it was quite clear to him that he had realised all this that very morning – or was it the morning before? Above Glenmanus Wood, just at the moment when the door of that old house opened, and a girl dressed in white appeared, a girl to whom it all meant nothing, nothing but that a column of irregulars was somewhere in the neighbourhood and being chased off by soldiers. At that very moment he had felt something explode within him at the inhumanity, the coldness, of it all. He had wanted to wave to her; what was that but the desire for some human contact? And then the presence of immediate danger and the necessity for flight had driven it out of his mind, but now it returned with all the dark power of nocturnal melancholy surging up beneath it; the feeling of his own loneliness, his own unimportance, his own folly.

"What use is it all?" he asked himself aloud, and the wind answered with a low, long-ebbing sound, a murmur, hushed and sustained, that seemed to penetrate the old house and become portion of its secret grief.

He felt his companion stir beside him in the bed. Then Keown sat up. He sat there for a long while silent, and Hickey, fearing the intrusion of his speech lay still and closed his eyes. At last Keown spoke, and his voice startled Hickey by its note of vibrant horror.

"Jim!"

"I musn't answer," thought Hickey.

"Jim!" A hand felt about the bed for him and closed on his arm.

"Jim, Jim! Wake up! Listen to me!"

"Well?"

"Do you hear it?"

"What?"

"Listen!"

"Do you mean the wind?"

"Jim!"

"Oh, do for Heaven's sake go to sleep!"

"Listen to that, Jim!"

"I'm listening!"

"Oh, my God! There it is again!"

The wind. It kept up that steady murmur that filled the old house like the bellows filling an organ. Then a clear, startling note rose above the light monotone, and the boards creaked, and the windows strained, and the trees shook with the noise of a breaking wave.

"Jim, I say!"

"Well, what is it?"

"Christ Almightly, man, I can't stand it!"

Keown tossed off the bedclothes, fell back upon the pillows and lay naked with his arms covering his eyes. Hickey started up.

"What's wrong with you?"

"It's them, Jim! It's them!" His voice half-rose into a scream.

"Shut up, do, or you'll wake the whole house! Is that what we came here for? Come on, out with it! What are you snivelling about?"

"I tell you they're outside. Don't you hear them, blast you?"

Hickey's hand closed tightly over his mouth.

"Be quiet! Be quiet! There are old people in this house. I won't have them disturbed I tell you."

"I won't be quiet. Listen!"

The wind was rising again. Once it dropped at all it took a long time to mobilise its scattered fury. Hickey could feel the other man grow rigid with fear under his hands.

"Listen! Oh, Jim, what am I to do?"

"For the last time I warn you. If you don't keep quiet, so help me, God, I'll smash you up! You've drunk too much, that's what's wrong with you."

"Oh! oh!"

"Careful now!"

It was coming. The wind rose into a triumphant howl and Keown struggled frantically. He dragged at Hickey's left hand which tried to silence him, and his mouth had formed a shriek when the other's fist descended with a blow that turned it suddenly to a gasp of pain.

"Now, will that keep you quiet?"

Hickey struck again.

"Oh, for Jesus' sake, Jimmie, don't beat me! I'm not telling lies, it's them all right."

He was sobbing quietly. The first blow must have cut his lip for Hickey felt the blood trickle across his left hand.

"Will you be quiet then?"

"I'll be quiet, Jimmie. Only don't beat me, don't beat me!"

"I won't beat you. Are you cut?"

"Jimmie!"

"Are you cut? I said."

"Hold my hand, Jimmie!"

Hickey took his hand, and seeing him quieter lay down again beside him. After a few moments Keown's free hand rose and felt his arm and shoulder, even his face, for company. A queer night's rest, thought Hickey ruefully.

For him, at any rate, there was no rest. His companion would lie quiet for a little time, gasping and moaning when the wind blew strongly; but then some more violent blast would come that shook the house, or whirled a loose slate crashing on the cobbles of the yard, and it would begin all over again.

"Jim, they're after me!"

"Be quiet, man! For the good God's sake be quiet!"

"I hear them! I hear them talking in the yard. They're coming for me. Jim, where in Christ's name is my gun? Quick! Quick!"

"There's nobody in the yard, I tell you, and it's nothing but a gale of wind. You and your gun! You're a nice man to trust with a gun! Bawling your heart out because there's a bit of a wind blowing!"

"Ah, Jim, Jim, it's all up with me! All up, all up!"

It was just upon dawn when, from sheer exhaustion, he fell asleep. Hickey rose quietly for fear of disturbing him, pulled on his riding-breeches and coat, and, having lit a cigarette, sat beside the window and smoked. The wind had died down somewhat, and, with the half-light that struggled through the flying clouds above the tree-tops, its rage seemed to count no longer. A grey mist hugged the yard below, and covered all but the tops of the trees. As it cleared, minute by minute, he perceived all about him broken slates, with straw and withered leaves that rustled when the wind blew them about. The mist cleared farther, and he saw the trees looking much barer than they had looked the day before, with broken branches and the new day showing in great, rugged patches between them. The beeches, silver-bright with their sinewy limbs, seemed to him like athletes stripped for a contest. Light, a cold, wintry, forbidding light suffused the chill air. The birds were singing

At last he heard a door open and shut. Then the bolts on the back door were drawn; he heard a heavy step in the yard, and Sheela passed across it in the direction of one of the outhouses, carrying a large bucket. Her feet, in men's boots twice too big for her, made a metallic clatter upon the cobbles. Her hair hung down her back in one long plait of dull gold, and her body, slender as a hound's, made a deep furrow for it as she walked.

He rose silently, pulled on his stockings, and tiptoed down the creaking stairs to the kitchen. It was almost completely dark, but for the mist of weak light that came through the open door. When he heard her step outside he went to meet her and took a bucket of turf from her hand. They scarcely spoke. She asked if he had been disturbed by the wind and he nodded, smiling. Then she knelt beside the fireplace and turned the little wheel of the bellows. The seed of fire upon the hearth took light and scattered red sparks about his stockinged feet where he stood, leaning against the mantelpiece. He watched her bent above it, the long golden plait hanging across her left shoulder, the young pointed face taking light from the new-born flame, and as she rose he took her in his arms and kissed her. She leaned against his shoulder in her queer silent way, with no shyness. And for him in that melancholy kiss an ache of longing was kindled, and he buried his face in the warm flesh of her throat as the kitchen filled with the acrid smell of turf; while the blue smoke drifting through the narrow doorway was caught and whirled headlong through grey fields and dark masses of trees upon which an autumn sun was rising.

Machine-gun Corps in Action

When Sean Nelson and I were looking for a quiet spot in the hills for the brigade printing press we thought of Kilvara, one of the quietest of all the mountain hamlets we knew. And as we drove down the narrow road into it, we heard the most ferocious devil's fusilade of machine-gun fire we had heard since the troubles began.

Nelson slipped the safety catch of his rifle and I held the car at a crawl. Not that we could see anything or anybody. The firing was as heavy as ever, but no bullet seemed to come near us, and for miles around the vast, bleak, ever-changing screen of hillside with its few specks of cottages was as empty as before.

We seemed to be in the very heart of the invisible battle when suddenly the firing ceased and a little ragged figure – looking, oh, so unspectacular against that background of eternal fortitude – detached itself from behind a hillock, dusted its knees, shouldered a strange-looking machine-gun, and came towards us. It hailed us and signalled us to stop. I pulled up the car, and Nelson lowered his rifle significantly. The little ragged figure looked harmless enough, God knows, and we both had the shyness of un-professional soldiers.

What we saw was a wild, very under-sized cityman, dressed in an outworn check suit, a pair of musical-comedy tramp's brogues, and a cap which did no more than half conceal his shock of dirty yellow hair. As he came towards us he produced the butt-end of a cigarette, hung it from one corner of his mouth, struck a match upon his boot-sole without pausing in his stride, and carelessly flicked the light across his lips. Then, as he accosted us, he let out a long grey stream of smoke through his nostrils.

"Comrades," he said companionably. "Direct me to Jo Kenefick's column, eh? Doing much fighting your end of the line? I'm all the way from Waterford, pure Cork otherwise."

"Yeh?" we asked in astonishment, though not at the second clause of his statement, of the truth of which his accent left no room for doubt. He knew as much.

"Sure," he replied, "sure, sir. You have a look at my boots. All the way without as much as a lift. Couldn't risk that with the baby. Been doing a bit of practice now to keep my hand in."

"It sounded quite professional to me," said Nelson mildly.

"Ah!" The little man shook his head. "Amateur, amateur, but I must keep the old hand in. A beauty though, isn't she? All I've left in the world now."

He lovingly smoothed off some imaginary rust from his gun, which I took to be of foreign make. I bent out of the car to examine it, but he stepped back.

"No, no. Don't come near her. She's a touchy dame. Guess how much I paid for her? Two pounds. The greatest bargain ever. Two pounds! I heard the Tommy offering it to my wife. By way of a joke, you know. So I said, 'You lend me two pounds, old girl, and I'll buy her.' Nearly died when she heard I wanted to buy a machine-gun. 'Buy a machine-gun — *a machine-gun* — what use would a machine-gun be to her? Wouldn't a mangle be more in her line?' So I said, 'Cheerio, old girl, don't get so huffy, a mangle may be a useful article, but it isn't much fun, and anyway, this round is on me.' And I rose the money off an old Jew in the Marsh. So help me, God, amen. Wasn't I right?"

"And where are you off to now?" asked Nelson.

"You gentlemen will tell me that, I hope. Jo Kenefick's

column, that's where I'm going. Know Tom Casey? No? Well, I served under Tom. He'll tell you all about me, soldier."

We directed him to Jo's column, which we had left in a village a few miles down the valley.

"You gentlemen wouldn't have an old bob about you, I suppose?" he asked dreamily, and seeing the answer in our eyes hurried on with, "No, no, of course you wouldn't. Where would you get it? Hard times with us all these days. . . . Or a cigarette? I'm down to my last butt as you may see."

Out of sheer pity we gave him three of the seven we had between us, and, in acknowledgment of the kindness, he showed us how he could wag both ears in imitation of a dog. It struck me that it was not the first time he had fallen on evil days. Then with a cheerful good-bye he left us, and we sat in the car watching his game, sprightly, dilapidated figure disappear over the mountains on its way to the column. After that we drove into Kilvara.

At the schoolmaster's house we stopped to examine the old school which had been indicated as a likely head-quarters for our press. There Nelson set himself to win round the schoolmaster's daughter, a fine, tall, red-haired girl, who looked at us with open hostility. He succeeded so well that she invited us in to tea; but with the tea we had to win over the schoolmaster himself and his second daughter, a much more difficult job. Neither Nelson nor I could fathom what lay beneath their hostility; the family seemed to have no interest in politics outside the court and society column of the daily press; and it was not until the old teacher asked with a snarl whether we had heard firing as we came up that we began to see bottom.

"Ah," said Nelson laughing, "you're finished with the tramp."

"Are we, I wonder?" asked the teacher grimly.

"That man," said Nelson, "was the funniest thing I've seen for months."

"Funny?" exclaimed the younger daughter flaring up.

"I'm glad you think it fun!"

"Well, what did he do to you, anyhow?" asked Nelson irritably. Nelson was touchy about what he called the *bourgeoisie*.

"Do you know," she asked angrily, "when my dad said he had no room for him here with two girls in the house, your 'funny' friend took his trench mortar, and put it on a sort of camera stand in front of the hall door, and threatened to blow us all into eternity?"

"The little rat!" said Nelson. "And he actually wanted to stay here?"

"Wanted to stay?" said the daughters together. "Wanted to stay! Did he stay for a fortnight and the gun mounted all night on the chair beside his bed?"

"Holy Lord God!" said Nelson profanely, "and we without as much as a good pea-shooter on the armoured car!"

After this the story expanded to an almost incredible extent, for not alone did it concern Kilvara, but other places where the tramp's activities had already become the stuff of legend.

"He'll behave himself when Jo Kenefick gets him," said Nelson grimly.

"I tell you what, girls," he went on, "come back with us in the car and tell Jo Kenefick the story as you told it now."

At this the girls blushed and giggled, but at last they agreed, and proceeded to ready themselves for the journey, the old schoolmaster meanwhile becoming more and more polite and even going to the trouble of explaining to us the half-dozen different reasons why we could *not* win the war.

I have no intention of describing the journey to Coolenagh and back under an autumn moon – though I can picture it very clearly: mountains and pools and misty, desolate ribbons of mountain road – for that is the story of how we almost retrieved the reputation of the Irish Republican Army in the little hamlet of Kilvara; but what I should like to describe is Jo Kenefick's face when we (that is to say Sean and I, for we judged it unwise to lay Jo open to temptation) told the tale of the tramp's misdeeds.

"Mercy of God!" said Jo, "Ye nabbed him and let him go again?"

"But didn't he arrive yet?" asked Nelson.

"Arrive?" asked Jo. "Arrive where, tell me?"

"Here, of course."

"Here?" asked Jo with a sour scowl. "And I looking for him this fortnight to massacree him!"

"Damn!" said Nelson, seeing light.

"It was great negligence in ye to let him go," said Jo severely. "And I wouldn't mind at all but ye let the gun go too. Do you know I have seventy-five thousand rounds of that stuff in the dump, and he have the only gun in Ireland that will shoot it?"

"He said he bought it for two pounds," said I.

"He did," replied Jo. "He did. And my Q.M. came an hour after and bid fifty. It was an Italian gun not inventoried at all, and it was never looked for in the evacuation. Where did ye find him?"

We told him the exact spot in which we had last seen the gunner.

"Be damn!" said Jo, "I'll send out a patrol on motorbikes to catch him. That armoured car isn't much use to me without a gun."

But when we returned from our joy-ride at two o'clock the following morning – leaving, I hope, two happy maidens in the hills behind – the patrols were back without gunner or gun.

II

Three days later the gunner turned up – between two stalwart country boys with cocked Webleys. He was very downcast, and having explained to Jo Kenefick how he had been sent out of his way by two men answering to our description, he added, a moment after we had made our appearance, that he had been caught in a storm on the hills.

The same night it was decided to make amends for our previous inaction by attacking the nearest town, and that no later than the following morning. The men were hurriedly called together and the plans explained to them. The town was garrisoned by about forty soldiers and the armoured car, driven by me and manned by the tramp, was to prepare the way for the attack.

At dawn I stood in my overalls by the door of the armoured car and lectured the tramp. He was extremely nervous, and tapped the body at every point, looking for what he called leaks. I explained, as clearly as I could to a man who paid no attention to me, that his principal danger would be from inside, and showed him that my revolver was fully loaded to cope with emergencies.

We pulled out of the village and passed little groups of armed men converging on the town. I had to drive slowly, principally because it was impossible to get much speed out of the car, which was far too heavy for its chassis, and needed skilful negotiation, but partly because the lumbering old truck refused to work on reverse and, to avoid occasional detours of a few miles, I had to be careful to get my turns right.

Jo Kenefick, Sean Nelson and some others were waiting for us outside the town and gave us a few necessary directions; then we closed all apertures except that for the machine-gun and the shielded slit through which I watched the road immediately in front of me, and gave the old bus her head downhill. She slowed down of her own accord as we entered a level street the surface of which was far worse than any I had ever seen. As we drew near the spot where I thought the barrack should be I heard the tramp mumble something; I looked back and saw him fiercely sighting his gun; then the most deafening jumble of noise I have ever heard in my life began.

"Slow! Slow!" the tramp shouted, and I held her in as

we lumbered down the main street, letting her rip again as we took a side street that brought us back to the centre of the town. I knew that the enemy was in occupation of some half-dozen houses. Beyond this I knew nothing of what went on about me. The tramp shouted directions which I followed without question. "Slow!" he cried when we were passing some occupied post, and two or three times he exclaimed that he had "got" somebody. This was none of my business. I had enough to do at the wheel.

Besides I was almost deaf from the shooting and the chugging and jumbling of the old bus (all concentrated and magnified within that little steel box until it sounded like the day of judgment and the anger of the Lord) and suffocated by the fumes of petrol and oil that filled it. This went on, as I afterwards calculated, for at least two hours and a half. I could not tell what was happening between our men and the regulars, but I guessed that Kenefick would have bagged some of the supplies we needed under cover of our fire.

Suddenly, in the midst of a terrific burst of firing from the tramp, the engine kicked. My heart stood still. The old bus went on smoothly for a little while, and then, in the middle of the main street, kicked again. I realised that the only hope was to get her out of the town as quickly as possible, and leave the men to escape as best they could. I put her to it, stepping on the gas and praying to her maker. Again she ran smoothly for a few yards and suddenly stopped, not fifty feet from the barrack door as I judged. I let my hands drop from the wheel and sat there in despair. There was no self-starter.

"What's wrong with you, man?" shouted the tramp. "Start her again, quick."

"Are any of our men around?" I shouted, indulging a last faint hope.

"How could they be?" yelled the tramp, letting rip an occasional shot. "Nobody could move in that fire."

"Then one of us must get out and start her."

"Get out? Not likely. Stay where you are; you're in no danger."

"No danger?" I asked bitterly. "And when they roll a bomb under the car?"

"They'd never think of that!" he said with pathetic consternation.

I pushed open the door that was farthest from the barrack, pushed it just an inch or so in hope that it would not be detected. It occurred to me that with care, with very great care, one might even creep round under cover as far as the starting handle. I yelled to the tramp to open heavy fire. He did so with a will, and when I banged the steel door back and knelt on the footboard a perfect tornado of machine-gun bullets was whirling madly in wide circles above my head. Inch by inch I crept along the side of the car, my head just level with the footboard. My progress was maddeningly slow, but I reached the front mudguard in safety, and, still bent double, gave the starting handle a spin. The car started, jumped, and stood still again with a faint sigh, and at that very moment something happened that I shall never forget the longest day I live.

Silence, an unutterable, appalling silence fell about me, For a full minute I was quite unable to guess what had happened; then it occurred to me – a dreadful revelation – that I had become stone-deaf. I did not dare to move, but crouched there with one hand upon the starter and the other upon the gun in my belt. I looked round me; the street with all its shattered window-panes was quite empty and silent with the silence of midnight. I tried to remember what it was one did when one became suddenly deaf.

Then, the simplest of sounds, my hand jolting the starting-handle, roused me to the knowledge that, whatever else had happened, my hearing must be intact. To make certain I jolted the handle again, and again I distinctly heard the creak. But the silence had now become positively sinister. I gave the handle a ferocious spin, the engine started, and I crept back to the door on hands and knees. Still there was no sound. I raised myself slowly; still nothing. I looked into the car and saw to my horror that it was empty of gunner and gun. Then I glanced along the street and round the farthest corner I saw the last rags of my crew flutter triumphantly before they disappeared for good. The crew had gone over to the enemy, and left me to find my way out of the town as best I could.

I sat in among a heap of spent bullet cases, made the doors tight, and drove lamely out of town. Nobody tried to hinder me nor did I see any sign of our men; it was like a town of the dead, with glass littering the pavements and great gaping holes in every shop window.

I drove for half an hour through a deserted countryside until at last I caught up with a small group of men, two of whom were carrying a stretcher. I drove in among them and they surrounded the car, furiously waving rifles and bombs. For safety sake I opened the turret and spoke to them through that.

"Where is he?" they yelled, "where is he?"

"Where's who?"

"Where's the man with the gun. He hit Mike Cronin one in the leg, and if Mike gets him alive . . ." From the stretcher Mike fully confirmed the intention, adding his vivid impressions of us both.

At that moment Jo Kenefick and Nelson pushed their way through the excited crowd, and probably saved me from a bad mauling. But they were almost as unreasonable and excited as the others; Jo in particular, who promptly threatened to have me court-martialled.

"But how could I know?" I yelled down at him. "I couldn't see but what was before my eyes. And how does Mike Cronin know if it was a bullet from the car he stopped?"

"What else could it be?" asked Jo. "Where did you let that lunatic go?"

"He went over to the Staters while I was starting the car."

"Staters!" said Kenefick bitterly. "He went over to the Staters! Listen to him! And the last man evacuated the

82

town at four o'clock this morning."

I groaned, the whole appalling truth beginning to dawn on me.

"And the grub?" I asked.

"Grub? Nobody dared to stir from cover with that fool blazing away. And the people will rend us if ever we show our noses there again."

That was the truest word Jo Kenefick ever spoke. We did *not* dare to show our noses in the town again, and this time Nelson and I could be of no use as peacemakers.

III

A fortnight later and Jo Kenefick could talk about the affair; if he were pushed to extremity he could even laugh at it, but as his laughter always preceded a bitter little lecture to me about the necessity for foresight and caution, I preferred him in philosphic mood, as when he said:

"Now, you think you have a man when you haven't him at all. There aren't any odds high enough again' a man doing a thing you don't expect him to do. Take that tramp of yours for instance. That man never done a stroke of work in his life. His wife have a little old-clothes shop on the quays. She's a dealing woman — with a tidy stocking, I'd say. She kep' him in 'baccy an' buns an' beer. He never had one solitary thing to worry him. And all of a sudden, lo and behold ye! he wants to be a soldier. Not an ordinary soldier either, mind you, but a free lance; brigadier and bomba'dier, horse, foot and artillery all at once! What's the odds again' that, I ask you? And which of ye will give me odds on what he's going to do next? Will you?"

"I will not," said Nelson.

"Nor will I," said myself.

"There you are," said Jo. "My belief is you can't be certain of anything in human nature. As for that skew-eyed machine-gun man of yours, well, there's nothing on heaven or earth I'd put apast him."

Some hours later Jo's capacity for receiving shocks was put to the test. A mountainy man appeared to complain that the tramp was at his old tricks again. This time it was in connection with a squabble about land; there was a second marriage, a young widow, a large family, and a disputed will in it, but of the rights and wrongs of these affairs no outsider can ever judge. They begin in what is to him a dim and distant past; somebody dies and the survivors dispute over his property; somebody calls somebody else a name; six months later somebody's window is smashed; years after somebody's fences are broken down; the infection spreads to the whole parish; the school is boycotted; there is a riot in the nearest town on fair day; and then, quite casually, some unfortunate wretch who seems to have had nothing to do with the dispute is found in a ditch with portion of his skull blown away.

Not that we gathered anything as lucid or complete from the slob of a mountainy man who talked to us at such length. All he could tell us was that his cousin's house had been machine-gunned, and that, in the opinion of the parish, was carrying the matter too far. Nor did we want to know more. Jo Kenefick was on his feet calling for men when Sean Nelson stopped him.

"Leave it to us, Jo, leave it to us! Remember we've an account to square with him."

"I'm remembering that," said Jo slowly. "And I'm remembering too he got away from ye twice."

"All the more reason he won't get away a third time."

"If I leave him to ye," said Jo, "will ye swear to me to bring him back here, dead or alive, with his machine-gun?"

"Dead or alive," nodded Sean.

"And more dead than alive?" said Jo with his heavy humour.

"Oh, more dead than alive!" said Sean.

And so it was that we three, Sean, myself, and the mountainy man set out from the village that evening.

84

Three-quarters of an hour of jolting and steady climbing and we came to a little valley set between three hills; a stream flowing down the length of it and a few houses set distantly upon the lower slopes. The mountainy man pointed out a comfortable farmhouse backed by a wall of elm-trees as our destination. He refused to come with us, nor indeed did we ask for his company.

The door of the little farmhouse was open, and we walked straight into the kitchen. A young woman was sitting by an open hearth in the twilight, and she rose to greet us.

"Morrow, ma'am," said Nelson.

"Good morrow and welcome," she said.

"A man we're looking for, ma'am, a man with a machine-gun, I'm told he's staying here?"

"He is, faith," she said. "But he's out at this minute. Won't you sit down and wait for him?"

We sat down. She lifted the kettle on to a hook above the fire and blew on the red turves until they gathered to a flame. It was easy to see that Nelson, the emotional firebrand of the brigade, was impressed. She was a young woman; not an out-and-out beauty, certainly, but good-tempered and kind. Her hair was cut straight across her brow and short at the poll. She was tall, limber and rough, with a lazy, swinging, impudent stride.

"We've been looking for the same man this long time," said Nelson. "We've had a good many complaints of him, ma'am, and how he's caused more crossness here, we heard."

"If that's all you came about," she said pertly, "you might have found something better to do."

"That's for us to say," said Nelson sharply.

"Clever boy!" she replied with an impudent pretence of surprise, and I saw by the way she set her tongue against her lower lip that Nelson had approached her in the wrong way.

"That man," I said, "accidentally shot one of our fellows, and we're afraid something else will happen."

At this she laughed, a quiet, bubbling, girlish laugh that surprised and delighted me.

"It will," she said gaily, "something will happen unless you take that gun from him."

Her attitude had changed completely. Laughing still she told us how the tramp had arrived at her house one night, wet to the skin, and carrying his gun wrapped up in oilcloth. He had heard how her husband's people had been annoying her, had heard something about herself as well and come fired with a sort of quixotic enthusiasm to protect her. On the very night of his arrival he had begun his career as knight-errant by gunning the house of one of the responsible parties, and only her persuasion had discouraged him from doing them further mischief. Three times a day he paraded the boundaries of her farm to make sure that all was well, and at night he would rise and see that the cattle were safely in their stalls and that fences and gates were standing. It was all very idyllic, all very amusing; and as there is little sentiment or chivalry in an Irish countryside there was no doubt that the young widow liked it, and appreciated with a sort of motherly regard the tramp's unnecessary attentions. But Nelson soon made it clear that all this would have to cease. Nelson liked being a little bit officious and did it very well. Her face fell as she listened to him.

"Of course," he added loftily, "you won't have any more annoyance. We'll settle that for you, and a great deal better than anyone else could. I'll come back tomorrow and see you straight."

A few minutes later the tramp himself came in; it was amazing how his face changed when he saw us sitting there. Nelson was as solemn as a judge, but for the life of me I could not resist laughing. This encouraged the tramp, who began to laugh too, as though it were all a very good joke and would go no further. Nelson looked at me severely.

"I see nothing to laugh about," he said; and to the tramp: "Be ready to travel back with us inside the next five minutes."

"Let him have his tea," said the woman of the house roughly.

"I protest," said the tramp.

"It's no use protesting," said Nelson, "if you don't choose to come you know what the consequences will be."

"What will they be?" asked the tramp, beginning to grow pale.

"I was ordered to bring you back dead or alive, and dead or alive I'll bring you!"

"There!" said the young woman, putting a teapot on the table. "Have your tea first, and start shooting after. Will I light the lamp?"

"There's no need," said Nelson, "I can shoot quite well in the dark."

"Aren't you very clever?" she replied.

They glared at one another, and then Nelson pushed over his chair. We took our tea in silence, but after about five minutes the tramp, who had obviously been summoning up his courage, put down his knife with a bang.

"Gentlemen," he said solemnly. "I protest. I refuse to return with you. I'm a free citizen of this country and nobody has any rights over me. I warn you I'll resist."

"Resist away," growled Nelson into his teacup.

There was silence again. We went on with our tea. Then the latch of the door was lifted and a tall, worn woman dressed in a long black shawl appeared. She stood at the door for a moment, and a very softly-breathed "So there you are, my man," warned us whom we were dealing with.

"Maggie! Maggie!" said the tramp. "Is it you?"

"The same," she whispered, still in the same hushed, contented voice.

"How did you get here?" he asked.

"I'm searching for you these three days," she replied soothingly. "I've a car at the door. Are you ready to come back with me?"

"I—I—I'm sorry, Maggie, but I can't."

"Och aye, me poor man, and why can't you?" The hush in her voice, even to my ears, was awe inspiring, but he plunged recklessly into it.

"I'm to go back with these gentlemen, Maggie. By order——"

"Order? Order?" she shrieked, standing to her full height and tossing the shawl back from one shoulder. "Let me see the order that can take my husband away from me without my will and consent! Let me see the one that's going to do it!"

She threw herself into the middle of the kitchen, the shawl half-flung across one arm, like a toreador going into action. Nelson, without so much as a glance at her, shook his head at the table.

"I'm not taking him against your wishes, ma'am – far be it from me! I'd be the last to try and separate ye. Only I must ask you to take him home with you out of this immediately."

"Oh! I'll take him home!" she said with a nod of satisfaction. "Lave that to me." And with a terrifying shout she turned on the tramp. "On with your hat, James!"

The poor man stumbled to his feet, looking distractedly at Nelson and me.

"Anything with you?" she rapped out.

"Only me gun."

"Fetch it along."

Now Nelson was on his feet protesting.

"No, he can't take that with him."

"Who's to stop him?"

"I will."

"Fetch it along, James!"

"And I say he won't fetch it along." Now it was Nelson who was excited and the woman who was calm.

"There's nobody can interfere with a wife's rights over her husband – and her husband's property."

"I'll shoot your husband and then I'll show you what I can do with his property," said Nelson producing his

Webley and laying it beside him on the table.

"What did you give for it?" she asked the tramp.

"Two pounds," he muttered.

"Give it to you for ten!" she said coolly to Nelson.

"I'll see you damned first," said Nelson.

"Fetch it along, James," she said, with an impudent smile.

"There's a car outside waiting to take him somewhere he'll never come back from," said Nelson. "I'm warning you not to rouse me."

"Five so," she said.

"Go along to hell out of this," he shouted, "you and your husband!"

"I'm waiting for me own," she said.

"You'll get your two pounds," he said, breathing through his nose.

"Five," she said, without turning a hair.

"Two!" he bellowed.

"Five!"

"Get along with you now!" he said.

"I rely on your word as an officer and a gentleman," she shouted suddenly. "And if you fail me, I'll folly you to the gates of hell. Go on, James," she said, and without another word the strange pair went out the door.

The young widow rose slowly and watched them through a lifted curtain go down the pathway to the road where a car was waiting for them.

"Well?" she said, turning to me with a sad little smile.

"Well?" said I.

"Well?" said Nelson. "Somebody's got to stay here and clear up this mess."

"Somebody had better go and break the news to Jo Kenefick," said I.

"I can't drive a car," remarked Nelson significantly.

"It wouldn't be the only thing you can't do," said the young widow viciously.

Nelson pretended not to hear her.

"You can explain to him how things stand here, and tell

him I can't be back until tomorrow."

"Not before then?" she put in sarcastically.

"I suppose you'll tell me you haven't room for me?" he asked angrily.

"Oh, there's always a spare cowshed if the mountains aren't wide enough," she retorted.

So I took the hint, and musing upon the contrariness of men and the inhuman persuadableness of motors, I took my machine-gun and drove off through the hills as dark was coming on.

Laughter

While he was waiting for Eric Nolan to appear he told mother and daughters the story of the last ambush. It was Alec Gorman's story, really, and it needed Alec's secretive excited way of telling it and his hearty peal of laughter as he brought it to a close.

It concerned an impossible young fellow in the neighbourhood who was always begging for admission to the active service unit, always playing about with guns and explosives, and always letting on he was somebody of importance. The soldiers knew of his mania, and did not take the trouble to put him under arrest, much to his own fury and disgust. To anyone who would listen he told the wildest stories about his adventures, and pretended to any and every sort of office; he was quartermaster, company commandant, staff-captain, intelligence officer, and the deuce only knew what besides. And – the crowning touch in the comedy – he had a hare-lip.

Now, one night Alec had a private ambush – quite unauthorised, of course, like everything he did. He launched a bomb at a lorry of soldiers in the street, and then ran away up a dark lane, his cap pulled well down over his eyes, and his hand on the butt of his revolver. By the light of a gaslamp he saw Hare-lip running breathlessly towards him, in trench coat, riding-breeches and gaiters. When he saw Alec he stopped, and in a tone as authoritative as he could adopt demanded to know what was wrong. At this Alec's delight in devilment made off with his prudence. "There was an ambush at the cross, mister," he whinned. "Two fine boys kilt outright – they're picking up the bits of them still, may God punish the blackguards that done it!" Hare-lip stood for a moment as if stupefied. Then he clapped his hands to his eyes in fury and despair (it was a treat to see Alec take off this gesture). His hat fell off and rolled into a puddle. "Oh, nJesus!" he moaned. "Oh, nJesus, nand nthey never ntold nme!"

They laughed, mother and daughters. Stephen marvelled at the courage of the old woman who sat there so coolly while he cleaned his three revolvers. Every other day her house was raided, but crippled as she was with rheumatism, and with two sons in prison it brought no diminution of her high spirits. He liked to see her with a revolver in her hand, turning it over and over, and blinking endlessly at it, a good-humoured wondering smile on her toothless gums. Her younger daughter, plump and debonair, showed the traces more; she had begun to fidget, and her mother covered her with good-humoured abuse.

"I'm sixty-eight years of age, child! I'm forty-six years older than you, and a broomstick wouldn't straighten me back, but I'd make ten of you. Ten of you? I would and twenty! I'd go out in the morning with me little gun in me hand and stand up to a brigade of them. What did I say to their jackeen of a lieutenant the other night? Tell Stephen what I said to him. 'Get out o' me way, you rat!' says I, 'get out o' me way before I give you me boot where your mother forgot to give you the stick!' I did so, Stephen."

As for Norah, the elder girl, she was like a mask. That cold and pointed beauty of hers rarely showed feeling.

At last they heard Eric Nolan's knock. He came in, tall, bony, and cynical, a little too carefully dressed for the poor student he was, a little too nonchalant for a revolutionary. He smoked a pipe, carried a silver-mounted walking-stick and wore yellow gloves. There was a calculated but attractive insolence about his way of entering a house and greeting the occupants. He laid his walking-stick on the table, and covered the handle with his hat. Then he made way for Norah who went upstairs to dress, leant against the stair rail and made eyes at Mary whom he disliked and who heartily disliked him. Stephen, adoring even his mannerisms, smiled and tossed the three revolvers on the table.

"There!" he said, "these are ready anyway. Now what about the bomb, Mrs. M'Carthy?"

The old lady fumbled for a moment in her clothes and produced a Mills bomb red with rust. She could not resist the temptation to hold the grisly thing to the light and blink admiringly at it for a moment before she handed it to Stephen.

"Oh, God!" she exclaimed, seeing his hand tremble slightly. "Look who I'm giving it to. Lord, look, will ye! He's shaking like an aspen leaf." And she gaily hit him over the knuckles. "You're no soldier, Stephen. Steady your hand, you cowardly thing!"

At that moment they heard a fierce hammering at the door. Stephen was so startled that he almost dropped the bomb, but the old lady was on her feet in a flash. She snatched the bomb back from him and took up one of the revolvers.

"I'll bring these," she said tensely. "Mary, you take the other two. Hurry, you little fool!"

Bent with pain she was already half-way up the stairs. The two young men stood, one at either side of Mary, not daring to speak. She was leaning on the table, looking blankly down on the two oily revolvers which lay beneath her open fingers. She had gone deathly pale. The knocking began again, loud enough to waken the neighbourhood.

Rat-tat-tat!

"Mary, Mary, what are you doing?" the old woman's voice hissed down the stairs.

Rat-tat-tat-tat-tat.

With a slight almost imperceptible shiver, she lifted one of the revolvers and slid it down the bosom of her dress; she did it slowly and deliberately. After a moment the other followed. Eric Nolan went on tiptoe to the outer door, and looked back at Stephen who was standing in the kitchen doorway. "Ready?" he whispered, and Stephen nodded, too unnerved to speak. He straightened his spectacles with an unsteady hand.

The door opened, there was a rush of heavy feet, and a tall figure dressed in green uniform that was sodden and black with rain stood at the kitchen door. Stephen drew in his breath sharply, and stood back. The uniformed figure lurched helplessly towards him, and without warning Mary staggered and burst into a shriek of excited laughter. Stephen ran to her, and was just in time to put his arm about her and prevent her from falling. He heard Norah taking the stairs three at a time. Her face showed no surprise, but it struck him for the first time that it was a tired, rather dispirited face. With her help he carried Mary to her room.

When he came back to the kitchen the man in uniform was sitting on a chair beside the door; a great flushed face and fuddled, anxious eyes fixed abstractedly upon the opposite wall. Abstractedly too his great hand rose and smoothed down a long dribbling moustache. Eric Nolan stood silently beside him in utter mystification. Then with a supreme effort of will the man came to himself and glared at Stephen.

"I – I forgot me bracelet," he said weakly.

"Who in hell are you?" asked Stephen.

"Who am I? Who am I? There's a queshion t'ask! Young man, I'm the Seven Corporal Works of Mercy. . . . But I forgot me bracelet."

Nolan chuckled grimly.

"You're probably only one when you're sober." he said. "At the moment you're very drunk."

"Drunk? Of course, I'm drunk. But I'm not *very* drunk. You sh'd see me when I'm took bad!" He clucked his tongue in horror. "I'm a fright – a fright! Six stitches it took t'mend wan man I hit."

"What brought you here then?"

"Wha' brought——? I'm a friend of the family, amn't I? Wha' brought *you* here, may I ask?"

Norah came downstairs again, dressed for walking. Stephen looked at her and she nodded.

"Good night, Tom," she said to the soldier.

"Good night, Norah love! Good night! Good night!"

"Remember me to the other six," said Nolan amicably, taking up his hat and stick.

The two young men went out with Norah, and stood for a few minutes by the door until her trim little figure, battling with the rain from behind an unbrella, disappeared round the corner of the avenue. Then they followed her nonchalantly, buttoning their heavy coats up at the throat.

When they reached the road she was some distance ahead of them, and this distance they maintained discreetly. They passed a patrol which was walking slowly down the road with rifles at the ready, but they were not halted. That was the effect of Eric's yellow gloves, Stephen thought gleefully.

They reached the top of the dark lane in which Alec had met Harelip. Norah, who was standing by the wall in the shadows, handed them the bomb and guns, and with a cold "Good luck!" went on. Two other men who passed her coming down the lane raised their hats, but she barely glanced at them. Then the little group of four gathered together, and after a whispered consultation climbed over a wall at the side of the lane and made their way through tall wet grass to the back of a row of houses that flanked the main road. At one point a house had been demolished, and through the gap they had a clear view of a public-house on the opposite side of the road, its big front window lit behind red blinds. Somebody was singing there.

They knelt in the wet grass as they did at the back of the church on Sundays, putting their overcoats under one knee. Stephen glanced at his companions. It was as though he still saw them in the darkness and the falling rain; Eric Nolan, self-conscious and faintly sarcastic about it all; Stanton, the gloomy little auctioneer, who as he said in his pompous way did these things "purely as a gesture – as a matter of principle"; and Cunningham, the butcher, who wasn't in the least like a butcher, and bubbled over with an extraordinary lightness and grace that suggested anything rather than Ireland. Cunningham was a funk, and admitted to funk with great elegance and good-humour. The sight of a gun, he said, was always sufficient to throw him into hysterics, and this was something more than a good joke, because Stephen had seen him when his ugly, puckish face suggested that his imagination was strained almost to breaking point.

Yet, unlike Stanton, he would not have admitted that it was a matter of principle with him, and perhaps he was speaking the truth when he said that he did it for the sake of enjoyment. Otherwise, why should he have come out night after night with them as he did, good-humouredly letting himself be stuck for the riskiest jobs, and recounting next day how he had faced them armed with bromides, aspirin and whiskey?

For a full half-hour they knelt in the rain, not speaking, almost afraid to move. The rain penetrated their pants, and the wet cloth hugged their knees. Stephen smiled as he saw Nolan's yellow gloves hanging like dead leaves from his left hand. His own cap sent an icy drizzle down the back of his neck, and the peak becoming limper sank across his eyes, half-blinding him. He knew he would be in a foul temper when this was over. The rain fell with an intolerable persistence. In the public-house over the way, one song ended and another began.

Suddenly he heard a faint hum and stiffened. He drew his dry fingers across the lenses of his spectacles which were streaming with rain, and glanced at the other three. But whether it was his spectacles or his nerves that were at fault, he saw only three shadows that might not have been men at all. He could no longer distinguish them, and as he looked more closely, they seemed to dissolve and disappear into the dark and empty background of the fields.

He felt himself alone there, utterly alone. Once more he dabbed furiously at his glasses, and now two of the figures took shape again and seemed to come to life for a moment. What he saw was the slow raising of one arm, then another; a hand shook and he caught the wet glint of a revolver. He drew his own revolver and looked across the road.

He could see nothing now but the red-lighted window opposite him that seemed all in a moment to have become very small and far away. He levelled his revolver at that; there was nothing else at which to aim. Somebody was singing, but the voice grew fainter as the *rum-brum-brum* of a heavy lorry lurching through the waste mud approached. *Rum-brum* – it came nearer and nearer – *brum* – and suddenly panic seized him. Suppose the lorry were to pass? Suppose that already it had passed unseen? He looked for his companions, but could see nothing except a billowing curtain of darkness on either hand; the red light of the public-house window had blinded him to everything else.

He half-raised himself; the red light went out; the singing continued faintly over the roar of an engine. He sprang to his feet. It took him but the fraction of a second to realise what had happened, and he fired blindly at the spot where the light had been. He fired again, heard a steady sputter of shots beside him, and a dark figure detached itself from the blackness around, and sped away through the thick grass. The song ceased sharply. The light appeared again, but now it was so close he felt he could almost touch it with his hand. He caught his breath sharply and wondered whether the bomb had been a dud or Cunningham had failed to draw the rusty old pin.

On the instant it exploded, but not close to him like the shots; he had forgotten it must burst on the car which had already rounded the corner. The sudden thunder-clap of it left him dazed; he stood for a moment and listened, but heard nothing except the roar of the engine as the lorry made off wildly and unsteadily towards the barrack. His sense of time had vanished. It had been merely the boom of the gong, the rising of the curtain. He waited.

Already, he could hear in the distance the sound of another lorry tearing up the road. He no longer wished to go, but felt as if he were rooted to the spot. It had happened too quickly to be taken in; he wanted more of it, and still more until the flavour of it was on his tongue. Then a hand caught at his arm, and giving way to the sweet sensation of flight, he ran arm-in-arm with Cunningham. He heard beside him something that was like sobbing, the throaty sobbing of hysteria, and had almost given way to his surprise and consternation before he realised what it was. Not sobbing, but chuckling, a quiet contented chuckling, like a lover's laughter in a dark lane. In spite of himself he found the mirth contagious, and chuckled too. There was something strange in that laughter, something out of another world, inhuman and sprightly, as though some gay spirit were breathing through them both.

They cleared the wall, rejoined their companions, and resumed their flight at a jog-trot. Eric Nolan was saying indignantly between panting breaths, "It wouldn't work! The damned thing wouldn't fire! I think it – a shame to – send men out – with guns – like that!" But passing under a street-lamp that was pale in the streaming rain, Stephen saw Cunningham's ugly wet face, flushed with laughter, running beside him and chuckled again. At that moment a dark figure detached itself from the gloom of an archway and came towards them. It was an old woman. She had a tattered coat over her head, and held it tightly beneath her chin; little wisps of grey hair emerged all round it and hung limp with rain. She was very small and very old. Stanton and Nolan went on, but Cunningham and Stephen halted to speak to her. They were above the city now, and it lay far beneath them in the hollow, a little bowl of smudgy, yellow light.

"Tell me, *a ghile*" (that is "O Brightness"), the old woman cried in a high cracked voice, "tell me, child! I heard shooting below be the cross. Is it the fighting is on?"

"No, mother," shouted Cunningham, and it seemed to Stephen that he could no longer control himself. He shook with laughter and looked at the old tramp woman with wild, happy eyes. "That was no shooting!"

"Wasn't it, son?" she asked doubtfully. "Lord! oh, Lord! I thought I heard shooting, and says I to meself, 'God direct me,' says I like that, 'will I risk trapsing down to th' ould doss at all?' And sure then I says, 'Wouldn't it be better for you, Moll Clancy, to be shot quick and clane than to die of rheumatics in a mouldy ditch?' And you say they were no shots, child?"

"No, I tell you," he shouted, catching the old tramp affectionately by the shoulders and shaking her. "Now listen to me, mother, and I'll tell you how it happened. It was an old woman was the cause of it all. The old woman in the shop below, mother. She's deaf, do you hear me? Stone-deaf, and that's how she spends the winter nights, blowing paper bags!"

She looked at him for a moment and laughed, a high cracked laugh that shook her tiny frame.

"Ah, you devil! You young devil!" she cried gaily.

"Good night, mother!" he shouted and strode on.

"Young devil! Young devil!" she yelled merrily after him, and for a little while she stood watching, until their boyish figures disappeared under the gloom of the trees, and the sound of their running feet died away in the distance. Then, still smiling, she resumed her way into the sleeping city.

Jo

Say what you like, boys, the war with England was only a squabble between friends. A squabble that is beside our war. For I seen both, and believe me, they were won and lost by different men. . . . Let me give you an example.

When the first draft was setting out for Limerick I noted the Marshal amongst them. Now, the Marshal was not one of our lads; he was the son of a British soldier who lived close by Cork Barracks. He had never done a day's honest work to my knowledge, nor to anyone else's, and though I have no desire to speak ill of the dead, he wasn't the sort of man that people like you or me would care to chum up with. But, of course, I had nothing to say to that. He joined the colours with the rest, and in a few day's time went off to Limerick with a good soldier's rifle in his fist. I don't know that he could even use the same – with ability, I mean.

Sitting beside him on the lorry was our Jo – Jo Kiely that is. Jo was a tall, thin, pasty-faced lad with high cheek-bones, that used to work in the haberdashery – he's in America now, so I can freely tell the tale. Jo and myself were always good pals, but all the same – I say this, remember, without malice – Jo was another of the latter-end-battalion. Speaking from memory, he was what you'd call a real, nice, good-natured fellow, though that free-and-easy smile of his had been spoiled by him having two front teeth knocked out in a tap-room row. There was a wild streak in Jo. Two nights before he joined, in the dews of dawn as you might say, didn't he knock me up with some daft scheme or other for stealing an express train and posting overnight to Dublin (where, you may remember, there was a big fight on). That was Jo, to the life.

I bid good-bye to the rest of the lads, and then I leaned on the edge of the truck and talked particularly to Jo. To the Marshal asking me did I think there would be much fighting in Limerick I naturally said I hoped there would, and the hell of a lot of it. A queer question that was for one soldier to ask another. Would there be much fighting? He didn't take his answer too well either, as I duly perceived by his face which was very fat and purplish-like, with big, raw, womany gills. So then the lorries whizzed off. I stood there cheering, and our lads all cheered, and Jo stood up in the lorry and blazed all round him with pure pleasure. But the Marshal didn't let as much as a squeak out of him, and I went away wondering in my own mind what had the likes of him out with the Irish Republican Army.

Well, as you may remember, the way we lost the war was the two sides coming to a treaty in Limerick while our lads were being blown helter-skelter out of the Four Courts in Dublin. So there being no war to speak of, the Marshal came home on leave in a day or two and then went back again. It was some time after before I was up their way. I was driving a Lancia car, and when I got as far as Kilmallock I seen it was only too true what we heard: that the truce in Limerick was after being treacherously broken and our army beaten out of the town. I drove into Croom that night, and found my own company stationed there, so when I gave them all the news from home I went off, very pleased to be able to spend the night with Jo. Strange to relate, I found him sleeping with the Marshal, and had, of course, to roll in, three together.

Next morning, when Jo and I went off to scrounge a packet of Scottish Field from the Quartermaster, I remarked in confidence it was a surprise to see him so pally with the Marshal — because the Marshal wasn't exactly our class — so it turned out that Jo knew the Marshal's father well, a really good sort though a bit gone on drink. Jo told me, too, in confidence that the Marshal was after making

101

well out of the Limerick joint, Jo having searched his kit at the time and found four watches and a dozen of silver spoons, not to mention other articles that weren't in the regulation equipment. This was no surprise to me, seeing who the Marshal was, and the strange fact that he asked for leave a few days after getting to the front; but, to be fair to all, I must say that you could never be certain of what you heard from Jo, for he had a strong imagination.

Anyhow, Jo was for keeping a quiet eye on him – because there were some things Jo wouldn't put up with, and that was one – but, otherwise, they were good pals. The same night Jo sniped a bottle of booze out of the local public, and the three of us drank it together. Afterwards, I drove a lorry-load of prisoners home to the city, so I didn't see either of them again for a while. But I brought messages home for them, and had a long talk with the Marshal's father, who, as Jo said was a really good sort. He was in bad health, and had only six shillings a week pension from the British Army, and his wife drank, so you can imagine what an unpleasant thing it was for me to go there at all: still they brought in a half-dozen of stout while I was there, and the father said (which was only right) that his feelings had always been with our lads, and that he was proud of the Marshal having fighting blood in him, as he said.

After this Jo and the Marshal and the rest of our lads came back, and they were in the fighting at Passage when the other side landed. We lost the war again at Passage – the most lamentable day of my life, I must admit, because my best pal was killed there, and because our lads, that were as fine a lot of soldiers as ever did right wheel on a parade ground, were being blown right and left like sheep without a shepherd. When I reported at the barracks for instructions I seen clearly what a hopeless mess we were in, with our rotten Commandant astray in his wits, shouting to all and sundry to escape, and our gallant Michael Desmond crying like a child because he couldn't stop the scare.

That evening, with my own hands I drove the last batch

of our lads out of the city; a lonely, lonely feeling that was, I remember, so that half the time I felt like crying myself. It was a hot summer's day and still bright daylight; far away on a hill-top you could see the Victoria Barracks sending up a blast of yellow smoke. As for the road, you couldn't keep your eyes open for dust, and at every side of you was the baggage our lads had dumped out to make the cars go faster. God! they hadn't half the wind up, that misfortunate day! A lump as big as an apple used to rise in my gullet when we passed people on the road, and I seen by their smiles what they thought of us.

Jo was sitting beside me at the wheel, and every now and then he cursed something deplorable, and remarked how he had a revolver drawn to plug the Commandant, only someone dragged him off. But again Jo was like that, and though I felt for him in my heart I knew he was easily moved to believe he did things that he never did at all. He told me that the Marshal had whipped his kit and stopped behind, and was blaming himself that he didn't shoot the Marshal too.

We slept that night in the castle of Macroom and next day we were paraded by Michael Desmond and told to go back to our homes quietly. He spoke so well, and we all loved him so much, that we could hardly keep our eyes dry. When we were dismissed most of the crowd started out to walk the twenty miles back home, but Jo and I stayed on for the night, and to relieve our melancholy feelings, got mad drunk and proceeded to shoot up the town. I was told after that I split one man's head with the butt of my revolver.

I think now maybe our little spree did us good, for when we went back we weren't half as sick as some of the others; and Jo and I and two lads out of the company began chucking bombs at the other side and always went about with a Webley in our pockets in case we got a chance of hitting anything. We heard when we got home that the Marshal was after joining up the other side, and Jo blamed himself again that he didn't shoot him when he had the chance — a man, he said, that had disgraced our flag with theft and cowardice. But this time Jo was more easily consoled, because he walked back into the arms of a sweet little girl who thought him the finest thing God made; and, anyway, as we both agreed, the Marshal was no good to any side.

Jo was becoming very wild and, I must admit, a real good shot, which in such dangerous warfare as ours (a dead man being a dead man) is of more advantage than in open fighting. But we weren't such pals as we used to be before the girl came along, because he thought I was in love with her and would give him away to the other side just to get rid of him. He was real mad about that. This will show you what an imaginary man Jo was when roused. So he used to go off some nights from wherever we happened to be sleeping with a pal of his called Alec Gorman, who was as daft as himself, and do a job on his own, and myself and another fellow would then do a job on our own to wile away the time. This was not very pally as you will naturally remark, but it came about, as I tell you, through Jo's imagination.

So one night when we were sleeping in a cottage about five miles outside the city it came into Jo's head that fighting was better than lonesomeness, so he and Alec sneaked off on their own. After a bit myself and my pal noted what they were up to (because they had taken their rifles), but there was nothing to be done about it, so we turned in, taking a bed apiece.

It was long after daybreak when they came home. I was awake but I was so offended that I didn't speak to them at all. Then, seeing me so hurt Jo got into bed beside me, and as it was the first time he had done that for a month I felt a bit mollified.

After a while he turned on his side and whispered into my ear that he was very fond of me and wanted to be friends again. I was very pleased, and we shook hands heartily on it, he being, as I perceived, hot and excited; and he said he was sorry for the misunderstanding about the girl and about me not being with them, because the other side had come on them, and I couldn't wish for a better fight. So we solemnly agreed there and then never to go out again without one another.

I left before the others were awake that day, taking care not to disturb Jo, with whom I felt friendlier even than before the falling out. I had a bit of work to do in town seeing the Quartermaster, and lo and behold! what was my surprise to read on the paper that there had been a big fight on the railway line and that the poor Marshal of all men was killed. Of course, I knew it must have been Jo and Alec and some others who were on the job, but for all that I was very sorry for the poor Marshal, who, with all his fear of death, had not succeeded in escaping the natural end of man. That evening, being anxious to do the neighbourly thing, however strange it might appear, I went towards the barracks to tell his old father how sorry I was, when who should I see sail smiling down towards me but Jo! I will say for Jo that he was a real, daring man.

"Call me a hypocrite, quick, Jack!" says he.

"Hypocrite what?" says I, not understanding. "Do you know where he was plugged?"

"Did I plug him myself?" says Jo blandly.

Well, I looked at him and my mouth must have been fit to drive a carriage and pair through.

"Listen to me," says Jo, suddenly becoming serious and pulling me in as his way was till he had me against the wall.

"This morning we stopped on the way out for a drink, Alec and myself. It was damn near dawn when we got to the railway line, too late to do much damage, so we agreed that as a matter of principle we'd just tear up a few of the rails. We were usefully employed on that occupation when about ten of the other side attacked us from the road. Alec ran up the cutting and the other side followed him, but I hid behind a clump of bushes, thinking no one would be left and that I could get to some commanding position and take them in the rear. After a few minutes, things having quietened down, I lifted my head, and if I did, a bullet popped by it as clean as tuppence.

"There was no trouble about getting away. All I had to do was to creep down the far side of the embankment, and skip off in the opposite direction. But I knew there was a man on the bridge waiting for me to appear, and at that minute it was as plain as the breaking day to me, that the man was the Marshal, and no one but the Marshal, and there was nothing in the world I wanted more than to put a bullet in the Marshal's thick skull. I made one run across the line to get at him, and he must have guessed who I was, for all at once he went wild and as I got close to the pathway by the bridge he leaned over the side and sent shot after shot down on top of me.

"Now, as I remarked, it was dawning day. The railway cutting was all foggy and dark (which probably saved my life), but there was a white light on the bridge, and when I looked up and seen his fat baby face all shaking with excitement and the bolt not slamming home quick enough for him, by God, I went wild too! Instead of climbing the pathway up the side I stood there on the rails and lifted my rifle as if I was trying to bring down a bird. I think the fool must have been half-mad with fright not to take cover, but there he hung over the top blazing away wildly and every second making him a more certain mark for the Angel of Death! I didn't even duck from one of his shots; I took my aim as cool and determined as if he was only a cockshot at a fair. I fired three times running, and before I could fire a fourth Babyface was down on top of me like a sack of meal. I had to jump out of his way or he'd have knocked me flying. He went bash between the rails, his cap sailed one way and his rifle another, and when I looked at him, I seen his head twisted skew-ways; he cracked his neck in the fall. But two of the shots had got him, brother, two out of three!"

"Did you look for the other!" says I, by way of no harm.

"Oh, two it was all right," says he, without a smile

"And how did you feel like talking to the old man?" I asked him after a while.

"I felt like hell," said Jo. "That was the worst of it. Somehow, I couldn't resist the temptation to say a word to him, and when he seen me what should he do but throw his two arms round me, and go on about having only one child and the Lord God taking him. Then he fell to crying and said I should have been there to save him. Imagine me saving him! I tell you I felt like hell because I'm fond of that old man!"

"And was the Mar – was the corpse, I mean inside?" said I.

"It was," said Jo. " 'Tis a nasty sight!"

"God rest him!" said I, meaning the Marshal. "He wasn't a bad sort himself."

"God blast him!" said Jo between his clinched teeth. "He was a bastard and an enemy of the Republic, and I swore to be quits with him. Go on in now before you're too late. They're drinking the dozen of silver spoons inside."

"I will not," said I a bit short. "I was only intending to be neighbourly."

On those very words we parted, and somehow I could never bring myself to be pally with Jo again. Though, as I said before, he was an imaginary man, and didn't always mean what he said, there was a terrible wild streak in him.

And after that, too, I never spoke a word to Jo's girl again.

Alec

When I came home from the column Henderson, the
Quartermaster, told me glumly that the only fighting man
we had left in our company area was Alec Gorman. The
company, that splendid company that had been trained to
form fours, turn, wheel, and march like regular soldiers,
the company was gone, and in its place a solitary
Cuchulain at the ford, stood Alec. Now, Alec had never
belonged to us, he was too much of an idler. Idler, lounger
at bars, tippler, scrounge, football fan, pry, gossip, and
maker of quarrels: that was Alec.

Every town has its own Irishtown and every Irishtown
its Alec. He was known to everybody. He was welcome at
every pub for miles around. Even the old women came to
him to take sides in their fights. For instance, when he passed Kate Nagle's door that old rogue would look out, or
mount the three-legged stool she used to look over the lane
wall with, and shout after him.

"Alec Gorman, how high up in the world we're getting! You passed me by yesterday without as much as
'Good morrow'!"

"Is it a man you want, Kate?" Alec would shout back.

"Ah, you blackguard!" the old woman would bawl
delightedly. "I'd get a better one than you in the Salvation
Army or the Incurable Hospital."

"You ugly old hake, and you're eighty if you're a day!
How well you wouldn't ask if I'd a mouth on me."

"Come in and search me, Alec boy."

"Will you give us a look at the old stocking?"

"Come in, come in, putty-nose!" And to crown it all Alec would go in and talk to her by the hour.

One night I was sent for by Alec to go to Miss Mac's public-house. We stood by the bar sipping pints of porter. He had dropped his voice to a whisper, and the crowd drew back as it were to leave us more alone. Alec was very tall, a splendidly-built boy with a long bright face, a nose that was a little flattened by nature (which caused Kate Nagle to speak of him as she did), and great, blue, wandering eyes. He wore an old navy coat and riding-breeches, leaned a little over his drink and me, and with one hand fondling the glass held on with the other to a revolver in his breeches pocket. Now and again he called a halt to fling a joke at the red-haired barmaid or raise a squabble with one of the men at the bar.

People came in and went out, old women with pint pots under their tartan shawls or little children with quart bottles wrapped in brown paper, and Alec spoke so low it was impossible to guess what he wanted. It seemed to have something to do with rifles that had to be shifted to a place of safety, but sometimes he called the rifles shovels, and sometimes butter-boxes (not to mention traps, yokes, and gadgets), and talked about a letter from the shop (which I took to mean Brigade Headquarters), and about the butter-boxes being in cold storage. He was also expecting Peter Keary, and he spoke Peter's name literally without a movement of his lips, watching all the time from under his eyes to see if anyone was listening.

It appeared, too, that during the evening he had found himself in fresh trouble. By his account Kate Nagle was standing quietly upon her three-legged stool to get a view into the roadway — at peace with the world as he said — when a quarrel blew up between herself and Najax opposite. Najax was a woman who leaned over her half-door a good deal; a pale, untidy, reckless, handsome woman with a wastrel of a husband and the temper of a fiend. Old Kate had been putting it about in her malicious way that

Najax was a Free State spy, and within five minutes the argument between them had drawn half Irishtown to its doors.

"We're short of men and we're short of guns," said old Kate, "but there's bullets enough behind us yet!"

What did that mean?, Najax asked the neighbours. What did it mean? Who were the bullets for? What were the bullets for?

"To give you and your misbegotten likes the hunt," said Kate in a solemn and reverent tone, launching a spit that reached to the middle of the road.

"Who'll give me the hunt, you old serpent?" screamed Najax.

"Ireland has friends yet, Norah Gillespie!"

"May the devil chase the friends of Ireland!" bawled Najax.

"May the devil chase the friends of Ireland – and your friends too, Antichrist!" bawled Najax. "You never had friends but for what they could get out of you."

Those were the words of Najax as reported to Alex by Kate Nagle. Innocent enough, you will agree, but Alec in his simple way went off into a rage. Who was the friend that stuck to Kate for what could be got out of her? Himself, of course, that was clear. Besides, it had been publicly wished that the devil might chase the friends of Ireland. What friend of Ireland was clearly indicated? Himself again. It was treason to the Republic and a libel on him. So Alec crossed the road to Najax's house, and stamped in on top of her, blustering and swearing. Najax retorted by giving him sauce. Then he lifted up a bath of sudsy water that was on the table before her and threw it at her head, leaving her with her own nightdress hung about her neck, dripping with water. The rest of the clothes that she had been washing he kicked all round the floor in a perfect fury.

This was Alec when he was quite himself.

Most of the men in the bar were British ex-soldiers. Since Alec was a child he had been listening to the stories they had to tell, stories about the wars in Africa and India and the big war in France. Now Alec had pushed them aside to make stories for himself, and they accepted the position without malice. I was listening to one of them crooning in a corner a song about the great war:

The troopship now is sailing, and my poor heart is breaking.
The troopship now is sailing, all bound for Germany . . .

when another came up to me and held out his hand.

"I knew your father, Larry," he said.

"Did you now?" said I, not knowing what else to say, and shaking hands with him.

"I did then."

"Go on now, Mike," said Alec. "Unless you're going to stand a drink."

"I knew his father," said Mike, turning upon Alec. "A good soldier of her late Majesty, God rest her! I knew the father and I know the son. I won't breathe a word, not wan word." He turned away from us.

"Aren't you going to stand that drink you bloody *oinseach*?" said Alec with a screech.

Mike turned round on us again and lifted his right hand high in the air — a royal gesture. He wasn't going to stand a drink, but he came back solemnly step by step while everybody in the bar looked on and listened.

"When I was in South Africa —" he said.

"Ah, shut up about South Africa!" said Alec. "What about the drink?"

"When I was in Pretoria, I went into a bar one day. There was three of us there. A bar, just like this. There is a young man behind the counter. 'This and that,' says Mackerel, one of the men that was with me, calling for the drinks, 'this and that.' The drinks are filled out. 'Where are you from?' says Mackerel, looking closely at the young man. 'London,' he says. 'Did you ever see this before?' says Mackerel, pointing to the badge in his own cap, it was the

Munsters' badge. 'Maybe I did,' says the other. 'Maybe you did too,' says Mackerel coolly. 'Where's that you said you were from?' 'London.' 'Say this after me,' says Mackerel—

'I have wandered an exile 'mid cold-hearted strangers, Far, far from my home and the beautiful Lee.'

'Go on now,' says the man. 'Say it,' says Mackerel sweetly. 'I will not say it,' says the other. 'Say it, I tell you,' says Mackerel, cooing like a dove. 'No,' says the other, 'I won't.' 'Do you know what you are?' says Mackerel in a flash, jumping the counter like a three-year-old, 'you're an informer from Ireland,' and, says he, whipping off his belt, 'so help me, Christ, you'll never leave this bar alive.'"

Just as he finished the story Peter Keary strolled in. He saluted everyone at the bar. The old soldier touched his cap and stood back.

"Evening, sir."

He turned to me again and went on in a whisper, "That's true, d'ye understand? True, every word of it!" Then he stood to attention and rapped out an order: "The Fusiliers will spring to attention, fix bayonets and slo-o-o-pe. Taking the word from the Brigadier." And still at attention he marched away to the farther corner of the bar.

There was nothing secretive about Peter Keary. He stood a little aside from us, and leant over the counter quizzing the barmaid. In a moment the atmosphere of mystery with which Alec loved to surround himself was dissipated. Peter was small, gay, and quizzical, with a diminutive puckish face and curiously flickering nervous eyelids.

"You're wanted at home, Alec," he said at last. "Ginger and I will be up after you."

Alec obeyed him, and shortly after Peter and I followed. It was a cold gusty night in early spring Between the public-house and Alec's home there were cottages at each side of the roadway, and, at one side there was a low wall and steps down into a little lane; it was from this that old Kate used to watch on her three-legged stool. The road before us was pitch-black, with only one lamp showing where the steps were. The cottages were white in the darkness, like snow or a very faint moonlight, and our feet started a metallic echo from the flagstones. I spun around when I felt the touch of a hand upon my shoulder, and had almost pulled a gun before I saw who it was.

But it wasn't a soldier, nor a plain-clothes man. It was Najax. Najax, whom I had not spoken to since I was a little boy at school, and she, a girl of seventeen, had been walking out with a colour-sergeant in the British Army. She had obviously been expecting me; her door was open and above the half-door one could see into her little smoky kitchen.

"Larry," she said shyly, "I want to speak to you."

Peter walked stolidly on, and I saw there was nothing else for it but to go in with her. She shut and locked the door behind us.

"Larry," she said in a low, bitter voice, "did you hear what happened me?"

On the table was a bath in which clothes (the same, I thought, as Alec had kicked about the floor on her) were steeping under a washing board. Najax's arms – fine stout arms they were – were bare to the elbows, and red, having been freshly dried, but I saw that she had been unable to finish her work, that her fury and humiliation had been too much for her. I said something about not minding these things.

"Alec Gorman came in and thrown that bath of water over me. As sure as God is my judge, Larry, he did; and I that never said one unkind word to him. Thrown the water over me and kicked all my nice clean things about the floor."

"Alec drinks too much," I said, "and when he has a drop in there's no answering for what he'll do. But he had no right——"

113

"And it isn't that I mind so much," she broke in, "but he called me -- he called me – a spy." She was scarcely able to bring out the hateful word, and looked up at me with blazing, reckless eyes suffused with tears. "In my own house he called me a spy. He was put up to that, Larry, he was put up to it, and it was that shameless jade across the way put him up to it, that shameless——"

And this time she was overtaken by tears, real tears, and sat down by the fire, sobbing fiercely with what the people call a *tocht* in her. Then as suddenly she stopped weeping, and tossing the dark hair passionately back from her eyes she looked at me with wild-cat determination.

"I've no one to avenge me, Larry," she said (she meant her husband, I knew), "and I'm telling you only because this night I'll go across to that wan and drag her from her bed and crucify her; and I'm telling you, Larry, because I may do her mischief, and you'll know why."

Her kitchen was bare and dirty; there was a ladder leading up to the loft; a strip of old curtain half hid the bedroom, in which a sacred lamp was burning before a picture of Our Lady of Perpetual Succour and casting a greasy light upon the pillows of the bed. Over the mantelpiece under which we sat was a picture of the Sacred Heart. The tiny window was covered by an old red petticoat, and in the light of an oil lamp bracketed to the wall the white room, with its deal table and bath, its hand-ful of plain chairs, looked hateful and bleak and sordid. And as I became conscious of it I became conscious of an intolerable feeling of pity in myself, that pity which is the curse of our garrulous and emotional race. She was look-ing up at me, haggard and fierce, and I was aware of the fine modelling of her nose and cheeks, of the hawklike in-tensity in her, and in a moment I was sitting beside her try-ing to soothe the wild look out of her eyes.

She was very like a child, and immediately began to cry, softly and without bitterness. I put my hand about her shoulder and began to tease her. My hand slipped from her shoulder to her waist. Suddenly she stopped crying, and taking my free hand in her two damp rough hands, she pulled the fingers this way and that, and told me in a voice half-broken by little sobs that she was no spy; that she had no sympathy with the boys, but wouldn't give one of them away for all the money of Ireland; that she had a cruel life; that she found it hard to be honest when she didn't know at night where tomorrow's dinner would come from.

Often I had seen faces like hers under a street-lamp on the bridge or along the quays. On some bleak and pelting night perhaps such a face would hurry past me, and I would stand for a moment leaning over the parapet. wondering what had driven that terrible look into it, until the face itself would emerge from the blackness of the water below and send me shivering homewards.

And so – my arm was about her waist, and when I rose to go she held it there with her hand, so that I had to walk to the door with her in that fashion. I was tempted to kiss her, but my eyes lit upon her long black shawl hanging behind the door and I remembered those faces upon the bridge. Instead of kissing her I made her promise not to fight the old hag opposite, and this she did with the same ready, childish acquiescence.

The night was cold and I ran until I reached the lane where Alec lived. He lived in a sort of lane off a lane, a tiny passage that contained one street lamp and one house. His sister opened to my knock, and going in I saw Alec and Peter at the table behind a barricade of washing. They were having tea, and I sat with them at the rough deal table and drank tea out of a soldier's ponny. The back door was open and Alec's mother was bringing in washing because the skies threatened rain.

I was bombarded with questions about Najax, and then Peter must be told about what happened previously. Peter was sore at it, and with his little face puckered up into a hundred wrinkles he began to remonstrate with Alec, but Alec had almost forgotten the incident and it was only when Peter called it a low-down trick that he began to defend himself. Then his mother (who felt it her bounden duty to join in any remonstrances addressed to Alec) left her work, stood at the foot of the table, and rubbing her hands in her coarse apron and wiping her almost non-existent nose, said:

"That's right. Speak to him, Mr. Keary, speak to him. And speak to him you, too, Larry. Indeed, it's a shame for him to do a thing like that to a woman that never said a hard word to him, and what will all the neighbours say about us, I'd like to know?"

But Alec told her in a cross voice to shut up for Christ's sake, and Peter realised the futility of saying any more.

After a while Alec and Peter went out into the yard, and through the window I saw them climb over the roof of the jakes into the field beyond. I was left alone with the mother and daughter. The mother was tall and like Alec in appearance, only her nose was phenomenally short and her jaw squarer and slacker. Everything she did was done in exactly the opposite way from Alec's; while every movement of his was vital she worked confusedly and helplessly. She cried frequently and drew her hand across the place where her nose should have been.

"Wisha, Larry," she said, "I dunno how 't'll all end, I don't so. And I can't talk to Alec, and I'm sure he'll do something dreadful on me one of these days. I brought him up hard, Larry, and I never grudged him the packet of cigarettes and the bottle of stout, but it'd be dreadful if he was swep' off to his death on me now."

"Shut up, maa!" her pretty daughter drawled.

"Why should I shut up, child? Sure, he never tells me anything he does except what I hears from the neighbours or what the soldiers tells me when they comes to the house for him. Oh, Larry, it does take the heart out of me when I sees them soldiers walking in with their guns and bayonets and bombs!"

"Oh, shut uuup, maaaa!" the pretty daughter drawled again.

"I won't shut up. Two packages of tea they stole from me the last night they were here, the blackguards, and a pound of cangles! And they tuk the pitcher of Alec in his first knickers, and when I told them how much the knickers cost me the sergeant said 'Well, ma'am, if it's any consolation to you, the pair he have on now is the last he'll wear in this world.' Oh, *Dhe*! oh, *Dhe*!"

She was sniffling miserably once more, her hands crossed upon her portly bosom when Alec came in carrying two rifles. He looked at her with growing rage.

"Lord God Almighty, that woman is bawling again!" he shouted. "Aren't you ever done whinging, huh? . . . Ach, go on off ou' that to bed. . . . Take your ma up to bed, Josie!"

"I suppose I'm better," his mother sniffed. "Is there anything else you want for the night?"

"There isn't. Did you get me the fags?"

"I did not. Couldn't you have got them yourself below at Miss Mac's?"

"Sure, they won't do me for the night, will they? Josie, run down to the corner shop for two packets of Woodbines."

"Gi' me the money and I will."

"Where in the name of God do you think I'd get the money? Here, ma, give Josie the fourpence."

His mother pulled out a dirty old purse from the pocket of her coarse apron and began to count the money. This was a cause of further sighs. Meantime, Peter had come in and he and I were examining the rifles for rust. And the clack of the bolts and the snapping of the triggers mingled with the clink of money in the old washerwoman's palm and Alec's audacious jests, when another voice joined in; it was the crotchety voice of Alec's father grumbling upstairs about being disturbed.

"Me peace of mind destroyed and me night's rest ruined on me," he was shouting.

Alec stood at the foot of the stairs and yelled up at him. "Ah, shut up you! Do you think you're in a mortuary chapel?"

"That's the way he speaks to his own father!" the voice

upstairs commented bitterly.

"A lot you have to complain of!" Alec cried gleefully. "Pity 'tisn't out in the middle of the Sahara you are."

"Bringing home rifles in the middle of the night when honest men are in bed!"

"Ay, then, and I'm only sorry it isn't a ton of dynamite I have until I'd blow you ou' that bed."

"Better fed than taught, that's what you are!" the old voice snarled down at us.

"Go on now, go on now!" said Alec with a roar of laughter. "If you're good, I'll take you out for a nice ride in your pram!"

The grumbling subsided into a moan and the heavy stepping of naked feet on the boards above. But Alec's mother, paying homage to a fallen majesty, spoke in a whisper; Josie was sent off for the cigarettes, and the old woman moved on tiptoe to the cupboard and fished out two candles. These she lit and fixed carefully on the table in their own droppings, and still on tiptoe with lips pursed up like a child she quenched the lamp. After a few minutes Josie came back, and the pair of them crept upstairs on their stockinged feet.

Peter and I were duly impressed by this dumb show, and for a little while talked in whispers, until some joke of Peter's sent Alec off into a shout of simple mirth; then we pulled our chairs closer up to the table and began to clean and oil the rifles.

II

We seemed to have been hours upon the road; hours, and we were dizzy with fatigue and our fingers clung to the cold rifles. None of us had a watch to measure the time by. We had smoked almost all our cigarettes, and tramped up and down the shelterless country road in the darkness. The night was cold and clear; the wind had dropped, and on the horizon a few, faint stars were burning. Suddenly we heard, dull and far away, a slight boom that seemed to come out of the very heart of the country. We stopped.

"There goes the bridge," said Alec. "Thank's be to Christ!"

"Give them a few minutes to get away," said Peter.

We listened in silence and once again we heard that dull reverberation, only more clearly because we were expecting it.

"You men can say what you like," said Alec, "but no barn will see me this night. I'm going where there's a bed waiting for me. Are you game?"

At that moment there were few things we should not have been game for. We followed him across the fields to a quiet suburban road on which there were a bare half-dozen houses, houses of the well-to-do people. Here among a mass of disused stables we tried to find a hiding-place in which to leave our rifles for the night. At last Alec hit upon the idea of putting them down a chimney-stack. If we had not been so confoundedly sleepy neither Peter nor I would have listened to him, but, because we were, he got his way.

Taking a ladder and a piece of rope he climbed on to the roof of the stables. I handed him up the rifles and he tied them together, dropped them down the chimney-stack — the fireplace, by the way, had been built across — and secured the rope to a nail inside. It was only after we had cleared away the ladder again that it struck him there was no protection for the rifles if rain came on, but by this time we shouldn't have minded throwing them into the river to get rid of them.

It was beautiful up there where we were. The whole valley of the river was spread out beneath us. The river itself, fringed by a few street-lamps, glowed here and there, and on its bank a factory and a railway station were busily lighted. Further off was the city, distinguishable by its massed lights that outlined on either side the two great hills flanking it. One could pick out certain familiar spots on the hills by the line that the winding street-lamps made.

As we turned up the avenue towards the house a dog began to bark; another answered him, and in a moment the whole place was a riot of yelping dogs; the barking came to us like an echo from very far away, and it seemed as if even in the city the damned brutes scented our approach. For the first time that night I was nervous, and tugged with all my might at the old house-bell. It pealed through the silent rooms within and wakened yet another dog who added his voice to the chorus. There was no other answer and we tugged again and again. At last we heard the pattering of bare feet in the hall. The door opened an inch or two and we pushed it in, on top of an old man who, with one hand, was holding up the breeches that sagged about his toes. I switched an electric torch in his face for a moment; a bleak, wintry, old face it was, the flesh converging in deep hollows to the unshaven chin, a toothless, snarling mouth and above it two sleepy, cold, blue eyes.

"We want a bed for the night, neighbour," said Alec.

"There's many wants beds that can't afford them. Who are ye?"

"Never mind. Any place will do us. I suppose we're late for supper."

"Is it the hunt is after ye?"

"Never mind, I say," Alec exploded, losing his temper.

"All right, all right."

"One good bed is all we ask. The master is away?"

"He is away."

"A sound judge, the master! There are a few things we'd like to say to him if he came back."

The old man showed us into a long low room lined with bookshelves. There were two beds in it, and with a sigh of relief Alec threw his cap on the dressing-table and began to unpin his collar.

"Ye'll be quiet now?"

"We'll be quiet, neighbour, don't you fret. You go and have a good sleep. And try to forget there did anyone call, because we'd leave more than a wife and children to regret us."

Old Rip Van Winkle pattered away. Alec having removed his tie and collar and boots, went heavily on his knees, and Peter after a little while did the same. Peter's prayers were short, and before sleep overcame me, he was lying beside me in the bed; but my eyes closed on Alec's devotions, and I remember him foggily with his eyes turned up to Heaven, beating his breast and mumbling fervent ejaculations.

When I woke it was morning and Peter had gone. I glanced around me; saw that Alec was asleep, and noticed with satisfaction the three revolvers lying on the little table between his bed and mine.

I dozed again and awoke slowly with an extraordinary feeling of oppression. The room was as still as before, but it was much colder, and as I opened my eyes I found myself staring blankly into the face of a man in civilian clothes who was sitting on the end of my bed, smoking a cigarette. Then I noticed that this strange man was holding a service revolver upon his knee, and a sick feeling of hysteria began to penetrate deep into my bowels. I turned my head cautiously and saw Alec sitting up in bed very wakeful, the clothes drawn tight about him. The room was full of men; I took them in one by one only to realise that I was lying on the bed with nothing but a singlet on.

"Well?" asked the man with the gun, and I could only grin vacantly. Then I remembered the three revolvers and realised that we would face the firing squad because of them. On the instant I was broad awake. I looked at the little table – the revolvers were gone! As if all too clearly reading what had been in my mind the man with the gun rapped out:

"Now, where's that gun of yours, Ginger?"

"Bloody well you know he have no gun." Alec had rapped out the reply before I could speak.

"Oh, no, he haven't," the other said mockingly. "Well, Ginger?"

"I haven't a gun," I said, taking my cue from Alec. A titter went round the room. But for the life of me I could not guess what had happened to the revolvers, and for a moment a delicious sensation of relief went through my body; but only for a moment, and again the misery of a trapped creature sank deep into my bowels.

"Get up!" one of the men ordered, and Alec and I got up and dressed. Meanwhile, the soldiers pulled drawers and bedclothes about in the search for arms, for arms that miraculously were not there. Then we marched down to the waiting lorries through lines of laurel and laburnum. There were more soldiers outside and we were greeted with cheers and jibes. An officer struck Alec on the side of the face with his clenched fist. These were only the details: as were the drive through quiet suburbs and early-morning streets, the clerks and shopgirls going to their work, the girl I recognised upon the pathway and in whom I said good-bye to everything I held dear – and how much dearer now – houses and people and things, home and work and pleasure, freedom certainly, perhaps life.

We were at the courthouse. We went up the steps; the clerks were turning in by ones and twos and looked at us curiously. We were taken downstairs and left in a filthy underground cell where five or six other men sat up and stared at us. Conversation was impossible, for one of the group was almost certain to be a spy. About an hour later Alec and I were called out together into the dark corridor and two or three officers set upon us.

"Where are the bombs, Ginger?"

"Now, Gorman, you'd better say where the dump is."

"We have no dump," Alec said sullenly.

"No dump? No dump? Where are the three skits you had last night in Norton's?"

"We had no skits."

"Oh no. And you had nothing to do with the bridges or the trapmine either? Mr. Peter Keary has told us about that already. Now, out with it if you want to save your skin!"

Peter? So Peter was caught too!

"If he told you all that why didn't he tell you the rest?" Alec snarled.

In an instant he was grovelling upon the ground with a blow from a revolver butt, and one of the inquisitors kicked him in the stomach.

"None of your backchat. You're for it. D'ye hear me? You'll get yours. Now where are those guns?"

Alec began to groan and the groan rose to a squeal as the officer kicked him again. The officer shouted at him to be quiet, but Alec only screamed louder, like a man who was in mortal pain; then I said something wild – I don't remember what it was – and found myself being throttled, while somebody hammered my head against the wall. It was all pitiably dark, and I could only see the shadow of the man who was throttling me.

We were chucked back into the cell, I without a collar and with the neck torn from my shirt; Alec whining and holding his stomach. When we got inside I put my hand on his shoulder and said something; he continued whining, and I was astonished at his softness. He threw himself upon a mattress in a corner, his knees doubled up to his stomach, and lay there, silent but for an occasional groan, until we were called out again. Then I began to get worried for him, because he had to be helped out of the cell and back, but if it served no other purpose it saved us from anything more serious than a chucking about and another throttling for me. That went on for the best part of the day; in the evening I saw a friendly face among the officers outside; an officer that had been in our battalion at one time, and succeeded in getting him to order our removal to the prison.

An hour later the prison gate closed behind us. As we walked in darkness up the old garden path and through the Governor's office into one of the halls of the prison I felt in my soul it was for good. At first I stood stupefied in the great circular pit, lit by hissing blue and yellow gasflares that flickered wildly in the breeze blowing through four barred gateways. An iron staircase up to an iron balcony with high barred windows and a circle of white faces; above that another balcony and more faces peering down at us through the half-darkness, that was what I saw. A

Dantesque vision. The flags under my feet were islanded by pools of rain-water, and in spite of the wind there was a stink of refuse and humanity.

From the balconies, each with its four great barred windows, long corridors of cells went off into the three wings of the prison. Alec and I were put into a tiny cell lit by a single gasflare; a cell scarcely big enough for one man, with an unglazed window next the ceiling. A man was sitting upon the floor hammering at a piece of bright metal on a metal rod. He was making a ring for his girl, he said, and it was a shilling piece which he had impaled upon the rod. After a while he got up and made tea for us in a dixie which he hung over the gasflare. Then we all went out on to the balcony for the saying of the rosary, and after that lay down upon two mattresses stretched upon the floor, and covered ourselves with a few blankets. When the three of us were lying close together we completely filled the available floor space though another mattress had to be left upon the waterpipes for a fourth man. After a time Alec began to shiver and complain again; he couldn't sleep, he said, and was very ill with the pain in his stomach. He went along the corridor to the latrine and got sick before he reached it. The other man, who was an ex-soldier, then insisted upon sitting up, striking a match, and showing us the wound he had received during the great war.

"You've nothing wrong with you as bad as that," he said angrily to Alec. "Look at me! Feel my ribs! Feel my ribs! There isn't as much as a pick of flesh on my bones from it!"

"Why don't you talk to the doctor?" I asked.

"He says I'm shamming, the blackguard!" said the ex-soldier settling down again with a groan.

I fell into a half sleep while the men on either side of me turned and twisted and sighed; when I woke it was to see a lantern shining upon me on the floor. It was the officer of the watch staging another capture – this time it was Peter. I sprang up and lit the gas. Peter wore no collar and his face was deathly pale. He sat down on the waterpipes with his head between his hands; then he took off his cap and I saw that he was wearing about his head a bandage, stained with blood. He was trembling all over and did not speak.

The sentry below bawled out to quench the light and I did so. Only then did Peter tell us what had happened to him. He had been captured by a second party of soldiers on his way in; they had taken him with them to where our fellows had laid a trapmine the previous night and tried to make him dig it up. But Peter had been fly and refused to dig; then they tried to make him run with the intention of shooting him as an escaping prisoner. He had refused to run and, in a rage, one of them had fired, wounding him slightly in the head. As he still stood his ground they brought him back, and that night, after we had left, hell had broken loose in the Courthouse. They had taken one man to the top of a flight of stairs; flung him down; prodded him with bayonets, and kicked him about the floor. Peter did not say much but we had good reason to know what he meant. Then, suddenly, Alec began to moan and shiver again, and I made Peter and the other keep still.

Next morning, to my great surprise, Alec woke in what, even for him, was high spirits. He went about the prison, chatting with everyone he knew and laughing boisterously. It was only after a while that I got him alone. He told me that on the previous morning he had pushed the revolvers in behind a shelf of books just as the soldiers were coming in the hallway. This gave me a fresh start.

If the old man had really given us away, as Alec suspected, he must find the revolvers sooner or later and perhaps send us before a court-martial. But it was no use telling Alec anything of that kind then. He was full of plans for an escape of all the prisoners. He had made them up during the night. We were to dig a tunnel or fight our way through the guard. It was perfectly simple, perfectly simple to himself. And it was only towards evening that the older hands succeeded in persuading him that one idea was as impossible as the other. Then he returned to the cell, looking wan and distraught, began to complain again of pains, and lay on the floor for hours without speaking.

Next day he looked so ill we called in the prison doctor. The doctor left some iodine and "black jack" (the only medicine he was ever known to administer). That day there were several rows between Alec and the original occupant of the cell, who was angry that the doctor had paid attention to Alec, and insisted on hammering at his silly old ring in the cell. He kept on mumbling indignantly to himself about shamming and malingering until at last Alec, in a towering rage, caught him in his two powerful arms, carried him out to the corridor, and swung him over the balcony rail, threatening to toss him into the suicide net. After this the ex-soldier refused to speak to any of us again.

Within four or five days I was shocked at the appearance of Alec. He looked like a man in galloping consumption. His cheeks had fallen in, he could not bring himself to eat, and now and again he rose and tramped fiercely up and down the corridor alone. When Peter and I approached him he looked at us blankly, as though he did not recognise us. Then he answered offhand and resumed his tortured walking. Every muscle in his face seemed to be drawn tight, and there was a glint of insanity in his eyes. Several times each night he woke us with his muffled shouting and groaning, and his powerful limbs tossed this way and that, in the grip of his dreams.

Another thing I noticed. He came to be too friendly with the officer of the watch, and after the count each evening, he spoke to him, sometimes in the cell, sometimes apart in the corridor. His overtures were marked; there was a whine in his voice, and he protested too much about his innocence. It was the officer of the watch who suggested to him that he should sign a declaration of allegiance, and, after a night of indecision that was a torture to Peter and me, Alec agreed. He signed, but that was all that came of it; those outside knew whom they had to deal with as well as we, and Alec remained a prisoner.

Then one evening, without a word to either of us, he disappeared with the officer of the watch. It raised no comment at the time, because men were frequently taken out to be questioned in that way, but Peter and I smiled at one another and shrugged our shoulders. We knew that Alec had agreed to show some of our hiding-places to the soldiers. And when an hour passed and Alec did not return we had to endure the questions of scores of men who hung about our cell, coming in, going out, passing a sly remark, and nodding their heads grimly. It was only when the ex-soldier, looking up from his ring-making, came out with the ugly word that was in all our minds that Peter lost his temper, and after that the squabble between them diverted us until midnight.

All next day we sat in misery, and the next, and the next. Then because in prison no mood can last for long without bringing disaster we both began to cheer up. I think the cause of the good humour on my part was a parcel I received early in the morning of the fourth day; it contained only a big wheelcake and a note.

"Dear Larry," the note ran, "I enclose a cake which I made specialy for you. I hope you will like it. Your poor mother is looking very well but she is looking very sad poor woman. I was glad to see One You Know at home again and he appolijised. He said you were speaking to him about me as well as Mr. Keary for which I am truly grateful. I hope in God to see you home again soon.—Yours truly, Norah Gillespie. X X X X X."

It was the first news we had received of Alec, and though it confirmed our worst suspicions, we were not angry with him. We were curious only to know what he had done or said to get himself out. We did not even blame him; we loved him too much for that, and in our hearts we know that he had done the only thing it was in his nature to do.

But this thinking of him, seeing him visit Najax and stand at the bar to drink his pint with the rest, stimulated our curiosity; not only did we want to know how he had bought his release; we wanted to hear him explain it all, word for word, to the neighbours, to old Kate, to Najax, to Mike and his companions — as we knew he would. In a way we were happy, as happy as we could be with those three revolvers lying behind a row of books in Norton's house, for these, as often as we thought of them, chilled us again. And that evening, as though to satisfy our curiosity, a fresh batch of prisoners arrived; amongst them a poor innocent from our own locality, a suspect. We fell on him together with our questions.

He looked at us in stupefaction. "Didn't ye hear?" he asked, and we were too wild with him to answer.

"Sure, God Almighty," he cried, "the whole world know of it by now. How he took them out some place there was rifles hid? In a chimney?"

"Yes, yes," said Peter and I together.

"And went up on the roof with them to show them there was no trap. And flung two of them head and neck back into the yard, and jumped clear off at the other side into a lot of bushes and brambles."

"Alec," said Peter, "our Alec. He did? He got away from them?"

"Of course he got away. He jumped from the roof in the darkness." The poor innocent raised his voice until it pealed through the corridor and brought out head after head to inquire what was up. "The grandest, the most desperate, the most magnificent escape ever made. He have a charmed life. Didn't I see him with my own two eyes swaggering about the cross yesterday with a gun in his breeches pocket? Didn't I? Didn't I see him drinking at Miss Mac's, and visiting the neighbours? Didn't I? More than poor devils like us can do without being caught. He have a charmed life I tell you!"

Visiting the neighbours! How like him it was, our own inimitable Alec.

Then Peter held out his hand to me.

"We're safe," he said in a low voice.

"We're safe," said I.

"And whisper," said the innocent, putting his arms round both our shoulders and winking solemnly to right and left. "I'll tell you something I wouldn't tell the others. Between you and me Alec is at his old tricks again."

"How so?" we asked.

"How so? Look here to me!" He pulled out a dirty copy of the newspaper for the previous day. "Read that and tell me in confidence what you think of it." He pointed to a short paragraph at the foot of one page.

"Dunmerial, the beautiful suburban residence of Mr Edmund Norton, was burned to the ground in the early hours of this morning by a party of men, wearing masks and carrying petrol tins and revolvers. The caretaker, Michael Horgan, an old man, is in hospital, suffering from exposure and injuries said to be the result of a beating. He is not expected to recover."

"There!" said the innocent with a triumphant glance, "there now! 'He is not expected to recover?' What do you make of that?"

Soirée Chez Une Belle Jeune Fille

This was Helen Joyce's first experience as courier.

On Tuesday morning one of the other girls passed her a note. The class was half asleep, the old professor was half asleep, and as always when he was drowsy his lecture grew more and more unintelligible. She looked at the slip of paper. "Call at the Western before 5 and say you've come about a room to let. Bring your bicycle. *Destroy this*." Conspiratorial methods – there was no reason why the message could not have been given verbally. "And may we not say," old Turner asked querulously, "or perhaps it is too serious a thing to say – though Burke – or it may be Newman – I have forgotten which – remarks (though he qualifies the remark – and let me add in passing that whatever we may think – and think we must – though of course within certain limits . . .)". The day was cloudy and warm; the lecture hall was suffocating, and a girl beside her was lazily sketching Turner who looked for all the world like an old magician or mediaeval alchemist with his long, skinny arms, flowing gown and white beard.

She called at the Western. Its real name was The Western Milk and Butter Emporium, and it was a little dairy in the slums kept by a cripple and his wife. Beside being used as a dairy and a political rendezvous it was also a brothel of sorts, but this she did not learn until long after. Low, dark, cobwebby, with blackened rafters that seemed to absorb whatever light came through the little doorway, it gave her a creepy feeling, "a hospital feeling," as she said herself. She looked about her at the case of eggs, the two shining churns of milk, and the half-dozen butter boxes, and wondered who in heaven's name the customers might be.

The cripple led her into a little back room, half kitchen, half bedroom, that was if anything lower and darker and cobwebbier than the shop; it was below the street level and was unfurnished except for a bed, a kitchen table, and two chairs. Here he produced the dispatch, and gave her directions as to how it was to be delivered. She paid more attention to his appearance than to his instructions. Somehow she had not imagined revolutionaries of his sort. He was low-sized almost to dwarfishness; his voice was a woman's voice, and his eyes, screwed-up close to her own, were distorted by convex spectacles tied with twine. He spoke quickly and clearly but with the accent of a half-educated man; she guessed that he read a great many newspapers, and probably had a brother or cousin in America who sent him supplies. At last he left her, sniggering, "to dispose of de dispatches as she tought best," but before she hid the tiny manilla envelope in her clothes she took care to bolt the door behind him.

Then she cycled off. The streets were slobbery and greasy. It was one of those uncertain southern days when the sky lifts and lowers, lifts and lowers, endlessly. But if the city streets were greasy the country roads were far worse. Walking, she was ankle-deep in mud, and when she stepped in a pot-hole she had to drag her foot away as though it belonged to someone else. Rain came on in spells and then there was nothing for it but to take shelter under some bush or tree. When it cleared from where she stood she saw it hanging in wait for her on top of the next hill, or above the river, or trailing in a sort of cottony mist along the blue-grey fences. And finally, when a ray of light did break through the dishevelled, dribbling clouds, it was a silvery cold light that made the ploughed lands purple like heather.

For four miles she met nothing upon the road but a wain of hay that swayed clumsily to and fro before her like the sodden hinder-parts of some great unwieldly animal. After that two more miles and not a soul. Civil war was having its effect. Then came a pony and trap driven by an old priest, and again desolation as she cycled into a tantalisingly beautiful sunset that dripped with liquid red and gold. By this time she was so wet that she could enjoy it without thinking of what was to come. She was tired and happy and full of high spirits. At last she was doing the work she had always longed to do, not her own work but Ireland's. The old stuffy, proprietary world she had been reared in was somewhere far away behind her; before her was a world of youth and comradeship and adventure.

She looked with wonder at the flat valley road in front. Along it two parallel lines of pot-holes were overflowing with the momentary glory of the setting sun. It sank, and in the fresh sky above it, grey-green like a pigeon's breast, a wet star flickered out and shone as brightly as a white flower in dew-drenched grass. Then a blob of rain splashed upon her bare hand. Another fell, and still another, and in a moment a brown mist sank like a weighted curtain across the glowing west. The bell on her handle-bars, jogged by the pot-holes, tinkled, and she shivered, clinging to her bicycle.

In a little while she was pushing it up the miry boreen of a farmhouse to which she had been directed. Here her trip should have ended, but, in fact, it did nothing of the sort. There was no one to be seen but an old woman who leaned over her half-door; a very difficult and discreet old woman in a crimson shawl that made a bright patch in the greyness of evening. First, she affected not to hear what Helen said; then she admitted that some men had been there, but where they had gone to or when she had no idea. She doubted if they were any but boys from the next parish. She did not know when they would return, if they returned at all, In fact, she knew nothing of them, had never seen them, and was relying entirely on hearsay.

Helen was almost giving up in despair when the man of the house, a tall, bony, good-natured lad, drove up the boreen in a country cart. "The boys," he said, "were wesht beyant the hill in Crowley's, where all the boys wint, and likely they wouldn't be back before midnight. There was only Mike Redmond and Tom Jordan in it; the resht of the column got shcattered during the day."

A gaunt figure under the gloom of the trees, he shook rain from the peak of his cap with long sweeps of his arm and smiled. Her heart warmed to him. He offered to lead her to Crowley's, and pushed her bicycle for her as they went down the lane together. "It was surprising" he said "that no wan had told her of Crowley's; it was a famous shpot," and he thought "everywan knew of it."

Crowley's was what he called "a good mile off," which meant something less than two, and it was still raining. But she found him good company, and inquisitive, as ready to listen as to talk; and soon she was hearing about his brothers in America, and his efforts to learn Irish, and the way he had hidden four rifles when the Black and Tans were coming up the boreen. She said good-bye to him with regret, and went up the avenue to Crowley's alone. It was a comfortable modern house with two broad bay windows that cast an amber glow out into the garden and on to the golden leaves of a laurel that stood before the door.

She knocked and a young woman answered, standing between her and the hall light, while she, half-blinded, asked for Michael Redmond. All at once the young woman pounced upon her and pulled her inside the door.

"Helen!" she gasped. "Helen Joyce as I'm alive!"

Helen looked at her with astonishment and suddenly remembered the girl with the doll-like features and fair, fluffy hair who held her by the arms. Eric Nolan, the college high-brow, had called her the Darling because she resembled the heroine of some Russian story, and the name had stuck, at least among those who, with Helen and her friends, disliked her. She was not pretty; neither was she intelligent: so the girls said, but the boys replied that she was so feminine! Her eyes were weak and narrowed into slits when she was observing somebody, and when she smiled her lower lip got tucked away behind a pair of high teeth. And as she helped Helen to remove her wet coat and gaiters the latter remembered a habit of hers that had become a college joke, the habit of pulling younger girls aside and asking if there wasn't something wrong with her lip. Not that there ever was, but it provided the Darling with an excuse to pull a long face, and say with a sigh, "Harry bit me, dear. Whatever am I to do with that boy?" She was so feminine!

She showed Helen into the drawing-room. There were two men inside and they rose to greet her. She handed her dispatch to Michael Redmond, who merely glanced at the contents and put it in his coat pocket. "There was no answer?" she asked in consternation. "Not at all," he replied with a shrug of his shoulders and offered her instead several letters to post. She looked incredulously at him, perilously close to tears.

She was actually sniffing as she followed the Darling upstairs. It was her first experience of headquarters work and already it was too much. She had come all this way and must go back again that night; yet it appeared as if the dispatch she had carried was of no importance to anyone and might as well have been left over until morning, if, indeed, it was worth carrying at all. She did not want to stay for tea and meet Michael Redmond again, but stay she must. Anything was better than facing out immediately, cold and hungry, into the darkness and rain.

She changed her stockings and put on a pair of slippers. When she came downstairs again the room seemed enchantingly cosy. There were thick rugs, a good fire, and a table laid for tea.

She knew Redmond by sight. The other man, Jordan, she had known when she was fifteen or sixteen and went to Gaelic League dances. He used to come in full uniform, fresh from a parade, or after fighting began, in green breeches with leather gaiters, the very cut of a fine soldier. The girls all raved about him.

He looked no older now than he had looked then, and was still essentially the same suave, spectacular young man

134

with the long studious face, the thin-lipped mouth and the dark, smouldering eyes. He was as fiery, as quick in speech, as ever. Eric Nolan had called him The Hero of All Dreams (a nickname which was considered to be in bad taste and had not stuck). In real life the Hero of All Dreams had a little plumbing business in a poor quarter of the city, was married, and had fathered seven children of whom three only were alive.

Michael Redmond, the more urbane and conventional of the two, was genuinely a Don Juan of sorts. He looked rather like an ape with his low, deeply-rounded forehead and retreating chin, his thick lips and short nose. He had small, good-humoured eyes and the most complacent expression Helen had ever seen upon a man. It was a caricature of self-satisfaction. About his forehead and eyes and mouth the skin had contracted into scores of little wrinkles, and each wrinkle seemed to be saying, "Look! *I* am experience." His hair was wiry with the alertness of the man's whole nature; it was cut close and going grey in patches. Clearly, he was no longer young. But he exuded enthusiasms, and talked in sharp, quick spurts that were like the crackling of a machine-gun.

Helen found herself rather liking him.

Jordan had been describing their experiences of the day and for Helen's benefit he went back to the beginning. While she was sleeping in her warm bed (he seemed to grudge her the bed) they were being roused out of a cold and comfortless barn in the mountains between Dunmanway and Gugan by word of a column that was conducting a house-to-house search for them. And as they crept out of the barn in the mist of dawn, their feet numbed with cold, they saw troops gathering in the village below with lorries and an armoured car.

Michael Redmond snatched at the tale and swept it forward. As they were making off they had been attacked and forced to take cover behind the heaps of turf that were laid out in rows along the side of the hill. It was only the grouping of the soldiers in the village street that had saved them. (He rubbed his hands gleefully as he said it.) Ten minutes of rapid fire into that tightly-packed mass and it had scattered helter-skelter, leaving three casualties behind. Long before it had time to reform in anything like fighting order they had made their escape. And they had been marching all day.

So being in the neighbourhood, added Jordan slyly, they had called on the Crowleys. Oh, of course, they had called! exclaimed Redmond unaware of any sarcastic intent on his companion's part. May would never have forgiven them if they hadn't. And he smiled at her with a carefully prepared, unctous smile that showed a pair of gold-stopped teeth and spread slowly to the corners of his mouth while his face contracted into a hundred wrinkles.

"Oh, everyone drops in here," tinkled the Darling as she flitted about the room. "Mother calls our house 'No Man's Land'. Last week we had — let me see — we had seven here, three republicans and four Free Staters."

"Not all together, I hope?" asked Jordan with a sneer.

"Well, not altogether. But what do you think of this? Vincent Kelly — you know Vincent, Helen, the commanding officer in M——— came in one evening about three weeks ago, and who was sitting by the fire but Tom Keogh, all dressed up in riding-breeches and gaiters, on his way to the column!"

"No?"

"Yes, I tell you. The funniest thing you ever saw!"

"And what happened?" asked Helen breathlessly.

"Well, I introduced them. 'Commandant Kelly, *Mr. Burke*,' and Vincent held out his fist like a little gentleman, and said, 'How do you do, *Mr. Burke*?' And after ten minutes Tommy gave in and said with his best Sunday morning smile, 'So sorry I must go, Commandant,' and they solemnly shook hands again — just as though they wouldn't have liked to cut one another's throats instead!"

"But do you mean to say———?" Helen was incredulous. "Do you really mean to say you don't bang the door in these people's faces?"

"Who do you mean?" asked the Darling with equal consternation. "Is it Tommy Keogh and Vincent Kelly?"

"No, no. But Free State soldiers?"

"God, no!"

"You don't?"

"Not at all. I've known Vincent Kelly since he was that high. Why the devil *should* I bang the door in his face? I remember when he and Tommy were as thick as thieves, when Vincent wouldn't go to a dance unless Tommy went too. To-morrow they'll be as thick again – unless they shoot one another in the meantime. . . . And you think I'm going to quarrel with one about the other?"

"Certainly not," said Michael Redmond with dignity. "No one expects impossibilities."

"Of course not," echoed Jordan, his voice tinged with the same elaborate irony. Obviously he was enjoying Helen's discomfiture.

"But what a ridiculous idea!" gasped the Darling as she poured out tea.

"Well, I don't understand it," Helen added weakly.

Whatever explanation she might have received was anticipated by a startling incident. They had noticed no previous sound before the front gate clanged open with a scream of hinges, and they heard the chug-chug of a car turning in from the road. The two men started up. Jordan's hand flew to his hip-pocket.

"Don't be silly!" said the Darling. "As for you," she added resentfully to Jordan, "you seem to have a passion for showing that you pack a gun."

His hand fell back to his side.

"Nobody's going to raid us. Besides, if they were, do you really think they'd drive up to the door like that?"

The car stopped running and she went out into the hall. Her reasoning seemed sound, and the two men sat down again. Jordan on the edge of his chair with his hands between his knees. They looked abashed, but did not take their eyes from the door.

There was a murmur of voices in the hall; the door

opened and again Jordan as if instinctively drew back his arm. In the doorway stood a tall young man in the uniform of the Regular Army.

"Don't be afraid, children," sang the Darling's voice from behind him. "You all know one another. You know Doctor Considine, Helen? — Doctor Considine, Miss Helen Joyce. . . . Rebels all, Bill! Have a cup of tea."

The newcomer bowed stiffly, sat down close to the door and accepted in silence the cup of tea which May Crowley handed him. He had a narrow head with blond hair, cropped very close, and an incipient fair moustache. He was restless, almost irritable, and coughed and crossed and recrossed his legs without ceasing, as though he wished himself anywhere but in their company. The other two men showed hardly less constraint, and in the conversation, such as it was, there was a suggestion that everybody had forgotten everybody else's name. The Darling prattled on, but her prattling had no effect and scarcely raised a smile. Even turning on the gramophone did not help to dissipate the general gloom. Considine looked positively penitential.

Suddenly, putting his cup on the table and pushing it decisively away from him, he said without looking round:

"I suppose neither of you fellows would care to come into town with me?"

A mystified silence followed his question.

"I'd be glad of somebody's company," he added with a sigh.

"But Helen is going back to town, Bill," said the Darling with astonishment.

"I doubt if she'd care to come back with me," Considine muttered with rapidly increasing gloom.

"Why shouldn't she? I thought you'd never met before to-night?"

The doctor ignored the insinuation, and turning to Redmond he went on almost appealingly.

"I'd take it as a personal favour."

"Very sorry," replied Redmond from behind a

suspicious smile. "I'm afraid it's impossible."

"What about you?" This to Jordan.

Jordan shook his head.

"Nothing to be afraid of, of course. I'd guarantee to bring you there and back safely."

Jordan looked at Redmond, who avoided the silent question, and once again, but with less decision, he made a gesture of refusal.

"But what in Heaven's name do you want him for?" asked the Darling. "It will take you three-quarters of an hour at most to get home. Less if you cross the blown-up bridge. At your age you're not afraid of travelling alone, surely?"

"I'm not alone," said the doctor.

"Not alone?" three voices asked in unison.

"No. There's a stiff in the car."

Fully aware of the dramatic quality of his announcement he rose in gloomy meditation, crossed to the window and spun up the blind, as though to assure himself that the "stiff" was still there. The others looked at one another in stupefaction.

"And how did *you* come by the stiff?" asked the Darling at last.

"A fight outside Dunmanway this morning. He got it through the chest."

His audience looked at one another again. There was a faint gleam of satisfaction in Michael Redmond's eyes that seemed to say, "There! What did I tell you?" The doctor sat down and lit a cigarette before he resumed.

He was all right when we left B——. At least I was certain he'd be all right if only we could operate at once. There was no ambulance — there never is in this bloody army — so I dumped him into the car and drove off for Cork. We had to go slow. The roads were bad, and I was afraid the jolting might be too much for him. I swear to God I couldn't have driven more carefully!"

He took out a handkerchief and wiped the sweat from his face.

139

"We talked a bit at first. He spoke very intelligently. He was a nice boy, about nineteen. Then I noticed he was sleepy as I thought, nodding and only answering now and again, but I paid no heed to that. It was only to be expected. It was getting dark, too, at the time, and I had to keep my eyes on the road. Then, as I was passing the cross a half mile back, I got nervous. I can't describe it — it was a sort of eerie feeling. It may have been the trees; trees affect me like that. Or the mist — I don't know. I called back to him and he didn't answer, so I stopped the car and switched on a torch I have (here he fumbled in his pockets, produced the lamp, and switched it on in evidence). Then I saw his tunic was saturated with blood. The poor devil was stone dead.

"So I'm in a bit of a hole," he added irrelevantly.

They sat still, and for the first time Helen heard the pock-pock of the rain against the window like the faint creak of a loose board.

"I thought there might be someone here who'd come into town with me. I don't like facing it alone. I'm not ashamed to admit that."

He was watching Jordan out of the corner of his eye. So were the others, for at the same moment all seemed to become aware of his presence. He seemed to project an aura of emotional disturbance.

"Well," he began hesitantly, seeing their eyes on him, "what can I do?" He gave a shrug that said the very opposite of what his face was saying. "I'll admit I'd like to help you. I don't want to see another man in a hole but — when the thing's impossible?"

"I'd bring you back to-morrow night."

"Of course. . . ." Jordan hovered upon the brink of an avowal. "There's another reason. The wife and kiddies. I haven't seen them now for close on three months."

"You'll be absolutely safe," said the doctor with growing emphasis. "Absolutely. I can guarantee that. If necessary I can even speak for the Commanding Officer. Isn't that enough for you?"

Jordan looked at Redmond and Redmond looked back with a shrug that seemed to say, "Do as you please." Jordan was alone, and knew it, and his face grew redder and redder as he looked from one to another. A helpless silence fell upon them all, so complete that Helen was positively startled by the doctor's voice saying, almost with satisfaction:

"Plenty of time, you know. It's only seven o'clock."

She looked at her watch and rose with a little gasp of dismay. At the same moment Jordan too sprang up.

"I may as well chance it," he said with brazen non-chalance, his hands locked behind his head and a faint smile playing about the corners of his mouth. "A married man needs a little relaxation now and then."

"Certainly," said Michael Redmond.

Though there was no sarcasm in the voice Jordan looked up as though he had been struck.

"You people know nothing about it," he said sharply, and wounded vanity triumphed over his assumed non-chalance. "Wait until you're married! Perhaps you'll see things differently then. Wait until you've children of your own."

He glanced angrily at the girls.

Considine waved a vague, disparaging hand.

"Why, it's the most natural thing in the world," he said, imparting a sort of general scientific absolution to the sentiment implied. "The most natural thing in the world."

The others said nothing. The two girls went upstairs, and while Helen changed back into her shoes and gaiters May Crowley sat on the bed beside her, and a look of utter disgust settled upon her vapid mouth.

"Honest to God," she said petulantly, "wouldn't he give you the sick, himself and his wife? Why doesn't he stay at home with her altogether? It's revolting! He should be kept with a column for five years at a time. He's been carrying on for years like that, skipping back like a kid to a jampot, and his poor drag of a wife suffering for him. There she is every twelve months trotting out in that old

141

fur coat of hers – the same old fur coat she got when they were married – and she has to face police and soldiers night after night in that condition! If they raid his house at all they raid it twice a week to keep her company. Because he's such a great soldier! Soldier my eye! If they only knew! But it is revolting, isn't it, Helen?"

"I suppose it is," replied Helen weakly.

"Of course it is. . . . Michael Redmond is more in my line," she went on as she stood before the mirror and added a dab of powder to her nose. "He's a man of the world if you understand me, the sort of man who can talk to a woman. I think I prefer him to any of them, with the exception of Vincent Kelly. . . . Now Vincent is a gentleman if you like. I'm sure you'd love him if only you knew him better. . . . But Jordan! Ugh! Thanks be to God, Bill Considine is taking him out of this. When he looks at you it's as though he was guessing how many children you'd have. He's a breeder, my dear, that's what he is, a breeder!"

Helen did not reply. She was thinking of the dead boy outside in the car.

"Helen, child," the Darling went on inconsequentially, "you'd better stop the night."

"No, really," said Helen, "I must get home."

"I suppose you must." The Darling looked at her out of indifferent, half-shut eyes. "Michael is a sweet man! . . . It's the way they hold you, isn't it, dear? I mean, don't you know immediately a man puts his arm round you what his character is like?"

When they came downstairs the others were waiting in a group under the hall-lamp; Considine in his uniform cap and great coat; Jordan looking more than ever like a hero of romance in trench coat and soft hat, his muddy gaiters showing beneath the ragged edges of his coat.

Michael Redmond opened the door, and they felt the breath of the cold, wet night outside, without a star, and saw the great balloon-like laurel bush in the centre of the avenue, catching the golden beams from doorway and window, and reflecting them from its wet leaves. The car was standing beside it out of range of the light. Helen stood behind for a moment while the others approached it, then fascinated, she followed them. Considine produced his electric torch, and a beam from it shot through the light rain into the darkness of the car. There was nothing to be seen.

Startled, the Darling and Jordan stepped back, and the little group remained for a few seconds looking where the grey light played upon the car's dark hood. Then the doctor laughed, a slight, nervous laugh, and his hand went to the catch of the door. It shot open with a click and something slid out, and hung suspended a few inches above the footboard. It was a man's head, the face upturned, the long, dark hair brushing the footboard of the car, the eyes staring back at them, bright but cold. The face was the face of a boy, but the open mouth, streaked with blood, made it seem like the face of an old man. There was a brown stain across the right cheek, as though the boy had drawn his sleeve across it when the haemorrhage began.

No one said anything; all were too fascinated to speak. Then Michael Redmond's hand went out and, catching the doctor's wrist, forced the light quietly away. It went out, and Redmond lifted the body and thrust it back on the seat.

"Now," he said, and the pompousness seemed to have gone from his voice. "You'd better start, doctor."

"What about you, Miss Joyce?" asked Considine.

"I'm cycling in," she said.

"We can pace you, of course. The roads are bad, and we shouldn't be able to go fast anyhow."

"Never mind," said Redmond roughly. "It won't take her long to get home."

Helen liked him more than ever.

He lit her bicycle lamp, and, with a hurried good-bye, she cycled down the avenue. She had gone the best part of half her way before the car caught up on her. Mentally she thanked Michael Redmond for the delay — "man of the world, man of the world," she thought. The car slowed down, and Jordan shouted something which she did not catch and did not reply to. It went on again, and his voice lingered in her ears, faintly repulsive.

The tail-light of the car (the red glass had gone and there was only a white blob leaping along the road) disappeared round a corner, and left her to the wet waste night and the gloom of the trees. Already the rain was beginning to clear; soon there would be a fine spell, with stars perhaps, but the road was full of potholes, and she could almost feel the mud that rose in the lamplight on each side of her front wheel, and spattered her gaiters and coat. And still the voice of Jordan lingered in her ears, and from the depths of her memory rose a bit of a poem that she had heard old Turner quote in college. Had he said that it was one of the finest in the English language? It would be like old Turner to say that. Fat lot he knew about it anyway! But it haunted her mind.

So the two brothers with their murdered man
Rode past fair Florence. . . .

The Patriarch

I

First, for that strange name of his. Patriarch was a laney malapropism for the name one would expect the old hero to be called; it stuck, and in its own queer way was most fitting. For if the old man was not really as old as it made him appear, he did seem to come to us out of another world, and spoke with a different voice, like the prophets to the people of Israel.

If I were put to it, I could mention a dozen ways in which he crossed my life, never leaving it quite the same. But it will be enough to describe how we first met; I but seven or eight years old; he already the patriarch of the long grey hair and blazing eyes who stood behind the counter of his little shop in the Marsh, selling half-ounces of tea and quarter pounds of sugar to the women of the lanes.

It was rumoured that he gave sweets indiscriminately to boys and girls who could speak a few words of Irish. That was the first I had ever heard of the language. I was hurt that this most practical of all subjects was ignored at school. Where was it to be learned? Who was it spoken by? Nobody, apparently; for nobody seemed to know. Then appeared one or two fortunate urchins, doves to the ark, who had been taught a few words of it in the Brothers' school on the quays. You said *cooooooooooooo* (just like that – very long-drawn-out), and mysteriously it meant a greyhound, or you said with a very broad "o" *boooooooooooow*, and it meant cow. That a cow could be called anything but a cow was not so understandable, for only the bigger boys talked backslang, and spoke of a "reyhoundgay" or an "owcay". Altogether it was a problem. My mother did not know it. My father, who had travelled even as far as Nova Scotia, did not know it.

Then someone remembered that an old grandmother whom I rarely visited was supposed to have heard it spoken in her youth at Aghada. I flew to her. O, yes, she had heard it spoken, and what was more, spoke it herself, more easily than English she assured me, but this I was not prepared to believe. My doubt sprang from her inability to teach it to me. It should have been so simple; I was prepared to devote a whole evening to it, yet she could do nothing except voice extraordinary combinations of sounds that merely made me laugh. No, my grandmother was not a success.

After trying in vain to teach me the Lord's Prayer and some song the name of which I have long since forgotten, she taught me with great difficulty to say "*A chailín óg t'rom póg, agus pósfaidh mé thu.*" With which sentence and its English equivalent I went armed on my first visit to the Patriarch's shop.

The visit was not quite the triumph I had expected. I was shy. I stuttered badly. I began by saying that I knew Irish. The Patriarch asked my name. I told him. No, no, that wasn't it; what was my name in Irish? I had never heard of my having any other name, but as the Patriarch seemed to expect it, and to look upon my not knowing it as culpable ignorance, I felt I was hopelessly in the wrong, and gave myself up to tears. It was only when I was restored with bulls'-eyes and acid drops that I could come back to my prepared speech, and then somehow I felt myself a little bit ridiculous. I was a wonderful boy, the old man assured me, but I felt ridiculous. It was only his asking me what the sentence meant that restored my confidence in myself. It was something, at least, to have a grandmother with whose aid you could puzzle heads as old as the Patriarch's.

"Young girl," I translated, "give me a kiss and I'll marry

you."

(My frivolous grandmother!)

At any rate she had now turned into a positive gold mine, and most of my spare time was spent about her kitchen. I learned from her, first my prayers, then various snatches of old songs which I got her to translate for me, more for the Patriarch's benefit than my own enlightenment.

I remember one fateful day when I went into the shop on the Marsh. There was a young man inside talking over the counter with the Patriarch. And when he saw me, the Patriarch began to speak in his vivid and moving way about Holy Ireland, and about the beautiful tongue in which our fathers had sent down their message of undying hatred to children forgetful of their fame. Made bold by his great words and those blazing eyes of his, I was induced to sing an Irish chorus that I had picked up from my grandmother. The old man listened in an almost ecstasy.

"Do ye hear it?" he cried as I finished. "Do ye hear it? The giants talking to the dwarfs!"

"What does it mean?" the young man asked him.

He shook his head in despair.

"I dunno, I dunno. For three years I tried to learn it, and sorra word of it could I memorise. Th' oul' head is gone on me."

"Oh, I thought you spoke it," the young man exclaimed, and the Patriarch's brow became gloomier and gloomier.

"I'd give five years of my life to know it," he said passionately. "The kings and priests and prophets of our race are speaking to us, they're speaking to us out of the mouths of children, and they might as well be speaking to that counter there." His fist crashed down on it.

"What does it mean, young fellow?" the stranger asked.

"Tell him, tell him," the Patriarch encouraged.

And I translated literally as I had heard my grandmother do:

"O, my wife and my children and my little spinning-

wheel. My couple of pounds of flax each day not spun –
two days she's in bed for one she's about the house, and
Oh, may the dear God help me to get rid of her!"

The young man laughed, or rather sniggered, profanely,
and I had a longing to fling something in his face. But the
Patriarch looked down on me with his bright despairing
eyes as on a favourite hen that had laid a robin's egg.

"Are you sure you have the meaning right, *a ghile*?" he
asked at last.

"That's what my grandmother says," I replied, feeling
that the next word would make me weep.

"Did she teach you ne'er a song about Ireland?" he
asked.

"No," I replied.

"Nor about Cathleen Nee Houlihan?"

"No," – I felt as if I were accusing her of some dark
treachery.

"Nor about the Little Black Rose?"

"No, sir, she did not."

"Begod then, but there's some meaning in that," he said
hotly. "Believe me," and he turned to the young man,
"there's a message in that you and I don't see. They wrapped up their meanings in dark words to deceive their
enemies."

The young man said nothing, clearly not wishing to hurt
him. The conversation – seditious no doubt, though it was
all above my head – went on. Suddenly the old man raised
a warning finger.

"I have it," he exclaimed solemnly. " 'Tis England he
means. The bad wife in the house. That's it – I have it all
straightened out now. You have to have them songs in-
terpreted for you. The pounds of flax she didn't spin are all
the industries she ruined on us. England, the bad wife – ah,
how true it is! Dark songs for a people in chains."

And so I went away, dedicated to the revolution, a
youthful carrier of sedition that was never even guessed at
by the poor country singer who had made my song. Still,
the old man did not fail to tell me find out if my grand-

mother knew the other songs he mentioned, about Cathleen Nee Houlihan, Kate O'Dwyer, and the Little Black Rose. But though she could give him some more difficult nuts of allegory to crack, that wedding song for instance:

Slattern Sheila was the cook,
And scabby goat's meat was the roast they ate,
And it stunk in a way you would not believe,
Because it was killed for a quarter.

of the others she had never heard in her childhood at Aghada, so I remained ignorant of those symbols of Irish nationality till I was much older.

But by that time, thanks to Michael Callanan, I already knew some Irish, and had imbibed a little of the old man's boundless hatred of what he called "the hereidhithary inimy."

II

Old Michael had a housekeeper, or, as we said, a woman that did for him, who was quite as unusual a figure as himself. She had been with him since she was a young girl, and that was a long time ago. She had at one period of her life spent a few months in an asylum, and people said this was Michael's only reason for not marrying her. I thought myself he might not have married her for the very sufficient reason that he was afraid of her. I was — at least in the beginning.

She was ugly, she dressed in the queerest old black clothes, and wore her hair in a fashion I had never seen on anyone else. Besides, she talked, or rather thundered, in an unnaturally passionate voice that terrified me.

But later on I discovered that this voice was not really her own, for one day, when she found out that I was fond of reading, she brought me up to her bedroom to show me her enormous collection of prayer-books and works of devotion. (I had forgotten to say that she was pious with an extravagance that fully accorded with her character). And while I sat on her bed, examining those books – some of them in a queer, crabbed manuscript – Ellen sang hymns for me or talked good-humouredly, quietly, and with a slight trace of melancholy.

I must say in Ellen's defence (if that excellent woman needs defence) that she was the first literary woman I met, and the best. When the old man was engaged, as he frequently was, in talks that I now know to have been seditious, I sat in Ellen's bedroom, on the edge of her bed, reading devotional works that I only half understood. I read there by the hour. My prime favourites were the penny booklets she bought in Church; things like *The Lure of Drink, Happy Married Life, How to be a Saint in a Bar-room*, and *The Miracles at Lourdes*. In those days nothing, not even the Deerfoot stories, gave me more delight, and today I can only look back with regret on the beauty and mystery of that infinitely moral literature.

There was the story of the drunkard, dead in his sins, who came back to earth in order to remove the decanter from the sideboard before his son returned, and who, being surprised at his task (probably more difficult for a ghost than for you and me), left the print of his fingers burned in the panel of the door. There is astonishing poetry in that one word "burned". And I recollect something that was supposed to be the true story of how Voltaire died, screaming for a priest – his name stuck in my memory because of the delicious thrills his hinted-at blasphemies gave me, and my delight in the propriety of his fate. Yet there are men and women in the world so barren of imagination themselves that they would rob the people of their heritage of imagination. Men and women like the Drake – but I am anticipating. The Drake has yet to be introduced.

These, then, are the two Ellens of my childish memory, the real Ellen who went on happily ironing and singing

"To Jesus' Heart All-Burning" while I read, and the public Ellen, tall, toothless and ugly, clapping her palms that gave off a sound like boards, and thundering "I tell you, Mrs. Clancy, St. John of Damascus distinctly lays it down. . . ." Her saints were always outlandish, and I begin to suspect the orthodoxy of her quotations.

There was one thing this curious pair had in common, and that was their opinion – mostly of politics. And lest you say the woman followed where the man led, I must add that the contrary was generally true. A full three days before Michael was ready to give his opinion on any subject, Ellen had already broadcast it.

Now this is a great gift – the greatest perhaps that God can give to any woman who has to live with a man from day to day. One could almost take out an insurance policy on the peace of a household if one could guarantee that a woman would anticipate her husband's opinion even by twenty-four hours. For eventually the man will be driven to suspect that truth (since a man's opinion is of necessity truth) originates with the woman, and before ever the horrid thought that she has led him astray can occur to him, she will seem to be leading him from his own errors on to her native path of righteousness.

Whether it was Ellen's feminine intuition that anticipated the laborious workings of Michael's mind or not, I cannot tell. But it is certain, that it took old Michael a full week to make up his mind about the rights and wrongs of the Great War, while on the very evening of mobilisation, when the Marsh was seized by an imperialist frenzy, Ellen was proclaiming at every street corner that "England's difficulty was Ireland's opportunity" – and getting stoned for her pains.

It was soon after this that I began to drift away for the first time from the Patriarch. My father and elder brother were in France, and the meaning of the lists of names my mother worked through with such suspense and anguish was gradually dawning on me. It was thought for her rather than any bitterness towards the old man that kept me away. He in fact had already made his own quiet compromise. He did not cease proclaiming his convictions, but he did not let them interfere with his own humanity. So, though he naturally rejoiced at every German victory, he was the first to sympathise with any poor afflicted creature of the slums who had been bereaved by it.

I like to think of the Patriarch, with all his hatred of England, as he was then; acting as go-between for the women of the lanes, reading their letters for them, filling up forms, writing appeals to Whitehall, applying for leave for men to come and visit sick wives and children, inventing sick wives and children for those who hadn't them, disputing pensions, allowances, and what not else. And the money that rolled in to him, bad debts from before the war, and the price of newer and bigger purchases made by women who before it had never changed a pound note – portion of all this was being steadily diverted to finance gun-running, or seditious newspapers, or Irish lessons for the few boys and girls who still wanted them! Yes, Ireland is a queer country, and it was never queerer than in those bad days before nineteen-sixteen.

Then came the bombshell of the rebellion. I cannot write about its immediate effect, because curiously it only affected me indirectly. The boys and girls about me buzzed with it; instead of stamps or birds' eggs they collected prints of the dead leaders or rebel ballads. But it did not touch me until one fine summer day when I was returning from the baths and saw old Callanan in a lorry between half a dozen policemen. He gave me the greeting I sought from him – I should have been broken-hearted if I had not had it.

I cannot describe the tumult of my mind that evening. All my old enthusiasms mounted like strong drink to my head. I rushed home and fished out my battered Irish primer, begged for pennies to buy picture postcards of Pearse and the other leaders, and began to furnish my bedroom with them. Down came "The Munster Fusiliers at Mons" and "The Irish Division at Gallipoli"; up went Pearse, McDonagh and Plunkett.

The Patriarch was not long in custody. It was his third spell in goal, I learned to my astonishment; for, of course, when he came out I lounged round his shop as much as ever before. The shop had now become a very important place, a sort of clearing-house, and every day scores of young men drifted in, leaned across the counter, and talked confidentially with him. There one was able to keep in touch with all the latest developments of the election warfare, reports of raids and arrests (as later on of ambushes and the number of casualties concealed under the official "our troops suffered no loss"); broad-sheet ballads, like "Who is Ireland's Enemy?" "Wrap the Green Flag round me, Boys," and "The Felons of Our Land."

Some of these I copied out and brought home with me. My mother read them with tears in her eyes. My brother back on leave from France copied them afresh, and took them to the front with him. He was killed there shortly after by a bomb explosion, and the ballads came home to us, torn by the splinter that had pierced his heart.

About the same time my grandmother died. She was very troubled towards the end by a confusion of her wits. Lying on her bed she recited long prayers in Irish, but she would be tortured by an evil imp that turned the prayers into "Vision-poems" and the Blessed Virgin into the spéirbhean, the sky-lady whose immortal loveliness was sung in sensuous rhymes by every Gaelic poet. This led to an occasional unintentional irreverence which troubled her more than it need have done.

On the day she died she asked for a mirror. My mother, after some hesitation and protesting, gave it to her. She looked at herself for a long while, fixedly and dispassionately, then she murmured, "Jesus, there's a face!" and handed back the mirror. She could not be prevailed on to speak for hours after, and that evening, just as dusk was falling, she gave a great sigh and died.

III

After this things seemed to begin again for my mother. It was as if she had exhausted her capacity for suffering with the death of Peter. My father had been sent back to England for good. Now she and I grew closer together. It was, I suppose, the combination of her piety and my patriotism that dragged us out of our beds at half-past five of a winter's morning to attend Mass for the souls of the men killed in Easter Week. Again I like to think of this period – how many grey, bitter-cold mornings we walked the streets of the sleeping city, and heard the dogs howling at us in the half-darkness. It became something of an adventure; the dogs' howling, the clang of our feet on the deserted flagstones, the shadows of solitary workmen, the dying blaze before a watchman's fire on the quays, the river when the gulls flashed out at us; cold, rain, that unearthly feeling of contemplation that the silence of houses gives; then the door swinging to behind us and shutting us into the warm, dim, smelly church with its pink and blue and chocolate statues, where a young priest said Mass for twenty or so other adventurers like ourselves; and last, the quick walk back through wakening streets to the little kitchen where a fire was set before us, waiting for the match and the kettle to crown it.

By this time the whole country was on the edge of a volcano, and the Patriarch was happier than he had ever been in his life before. He loved the sight of young men, and now he had young men in plenty to listen to him. He would shake me by the shoulder – I was then a gawky lad of sixteen – and shout, "Hurry up, hurry up, Dermod, will you! Hurry and grow up before we free old Ireland without you!"

It was through him I was put on volunteer work so young – dirty, rather useless work it was too, but for me full of thrills. Lounging round street corners, cap pulled over my eyes, hands in pockets, being smacked or kicked about by sundry spiteful old policemen, reporting at night to someone in Michael's little shop – oh, it was all thrilling

154

and wonderful!

And with it parades in the country of a summer's evening. Little parties of men scattered everywhere, falling in and tramping up long, summer-shaded lanes to a distant field that topped some hill; drilling under the sunset and the first dusk, doubling through the tall grass, and taking cover, soaked with dew, behind some hillock. And the early stars faint in the afterglow, the silhouettes of a half-company topping a rise, file by file, the flapping and cracking of signal flags; whistles blowing, illicit news-sheets being circulated, and the thrill of pleasure with which one was allowed, so very rarely, to handle a revolver. One is glad to have been young in such a time, not too young to miss being occupied with the mimic soldiering, yet not old enough to have had one's fancy rubbed the wrong way by it – just at the age when one's mind was ready for impressions, and when without all this it would have found no more to brood upon than books or games or a first love affair.

It was understood, of course, that I told my experiences to Michael. Even my secrets – for he was as excited over them as myself, and more discreet – such as the hour when Captain Maunsell, whom I was shadowing, went home; the house beside the barrack where I had found that a German rifle, in splendid condition, was kept; or where we stayed when some job forced us to sleep out.

We were innocent in those days, and yet strangely, when the armistice came and there was no longer anything for us to do, we woke and found ourselves hardened, almost grown up, a little sly, a little given to bragging, a little contemptuous of people like the Patriarch who indulged in what we thought false sentiment.

And this was how once again he and I parted company.

IV

While the Treaty squabble was on a group of us attended a party meeting. It was a pitiful business. There was sentiment by the barrel, lakes and rivers of sentiment. "Comrades who had fought shoulder to shoulder — must be no split — Ireland is — Ireland was — all personalities must be avoided." And a Free Stater rose to propose something or other in terms of such woolly sentiment that a republican rose to second it, and the first man rose to explain that he hadn't really meant that. And then one of our men walked up and laid a revolver on the table.

Immediately there was pandemonium. It was a declaration of war, and all the pious sentiments were forgotten while people shouted, thumped, and called other people all the ugly names they could think of. This was all that interested me, so I left. Michael Callanan was standing in the corridor. We shook hands, and I noticed that his hands were trembling. He dribbled profusely.

"'Tis an awful thing," he said heavily. "'Tis so. They used to tell us we could never agree, and now they're after proving it to us."

"It was bound to happen," I replied.

I was for saying good night when he asked me to come home with him. His house was lonely now, with no young men at all coming. It was a long time since I'd been to see them, and we might talk it over. Surely, surely, there was some way out, surely we could all join hands again? (All the old men talked like that.)

When we appeared Ellen pretended to busy herself in preparing the supper, but she was only waiting her chance. At Callanan's first sigh, she planted herself square before the fireplace, hands crossed upon her belly, chin lifted, while she laid down the law. She out-talked him every time he raised his voice in our defence.

"Believe me, Mr Callanan," she said with pitying scorn, "believe me, oh, believe me that you're worrying the heart and soul out of yourself for nothing! For less than nothing, Mr Callanan — for a pack of young pups without education or morals!"

"Oh, easy, easy, Ellen!" I cried.

"Pups!" she repeated triumphantly. "Vile pups! Miserable pups! The scum and dirt and leavings of Ireland! You'll remember my words, Mr Callanan. In the nobility of your heart you don't know who and what you're sacrificing yourself for, but when the public hangman has had his say with them, you'll remember what I'm telling you this blessed and holy night."

"Don't bother me, Ellen," he cried impatiently, "I won't hear a word agin them. They're fine boys, dacent boys, gentlemanly boys, all of them."

"Scum!" screamed Ellen again, throwing herself forward from the hips. With a massive gesture that consigned us all to the outer spaces of the universe, she opened wide her fingers and threw her hand out level with her shoulder. "They are cast out, body and bones," she intoned, "from the buzzum of my church. 'They live by the sword, and they shall perish by the sword. They shall not see my face, saith the Lord.'"

At this moment a woman rattled a penny on the counter, and Ellen went out to serve her. But when she came back she sat by the table and renewed her harangue. As she did so, one by one, and little by little, cups, plates, knives, forks, and spoons were pushed out of her way until a desert space of white cloth was cleared before her. This, we knew, was a certain sign of Ellen being in her theological tantrums. Old Callanan continued his protests, but they grew weaker and weaker under her relentless fire.

"Ellen," I said at last. "I know what it is. You think we're all damned."

"That is not for me nor for any mortal creature like me to say, Jeremiah," she replied coolly. "There is a Higher Judge whose judgments may not be my judgments. We are only poor, blind, ignorant creatures who must obey the laws laid down for us by Our Lord and the Fathers of the Church."

"The same laws," I said, flaring up without reason, "as ye invoked against anyone that ever tried to help ye."

"Those laws were never invoked without reason,

Jeremiah."

"They were invoked to destroy Parnell."

"Parnell have nothing to do with it."

"They were invoked again' the Fenians," said old Michael weakly.

"Individual opinions, Mr Callanan. Don't try to confuse me. Those were only individual opinions."

"And against me and my likes," I added, "for two years past."

"Which proves again that our spiritual directors can see farther than we can see," retorted Ellen, complacently rubbing her folded hands upon her belly.

"And against anyone," I cried, losing the last shred of my patience, "that ever showed a tack of intelligence or courage in a country where everyone of you is afraid to speak above a whisper for fear he'd be heard in Rome."

"Excuse me, Jeremiah Coakley," hissed Ellen, turning white with rage, "excuse me——"

"Be quiet, Ellen," old Michael interrupted suddenly. "Be quiet and make the tay. I'm tired. I think I'll go to bed."

"You'll go to bed now," said Ellen. "'Tis time you took your rest, you poor, misguided man. Come on with me!"

I was still more astonished to see him rise at her bidding. He bade me good night, apologising weakly for going, and I rose and saw him climb the stairs, holding tight to Ellen's arm. I went away, my tail between my legs, feeling indignant with the old slobberer. "To be led by the nose in that way by a woman!" I thought disgustedly. I forgot his seventy years and his days in prison.

V

And so the ding-dong of fighting went on. We – that is to say, the little group that had grown up under Michael Callanan's nostrils – managed to keep fairly well together. We never saw him now, in fact we rarely dared to go into

158

the city at all. After the first flush of enthusiasm has died away, fighting of this sort is a filthy game in which obstinacy and the desire for revenge soon predominate. Autumn dragged on into winter, and we still managed to remain intact.

Then one day, passing through one of the narrow streets along the quays, I saw Ellen. My slight disguise of spectacles and moustache did not deceive her. She put out her hand to stop me, while the blue hollows of her cheeks narrowed into a smile.

"Wisha, wisha," she exclaimed. "Is this Jeremiah I behold?" (She never would call me by the Irish form of my name, Dermod; there being no such saint — so she obstinately maintained.)

"Hullo, Ellen," said I.

"'Tis a cure for sore eyes to see you, Jeremiah."

"Ah, we know who you're glad to see nowadays," said I.

"Is that all you know?" she asked with an air of surprise. "Young man, don't ever dare to say the like of that to me again — the longest day you live."

"Is that the way with you?" I asked.

"Ah, lave me alone! Sure, them bishops would rouse anyone agin them! Why don't they preach what they were consecrated to preach instead of airing their opinions like a lot of old market women?"

"And the Patriot? What about him?"

"Wisha, th' ould fool, he'll get sense yet!"

And, of course, I knew before she said it that he would; but did that astonishing woman feel in her bones that Seumas Kelly, the youngest of our gang and Michael's favourite, would be dead within the next ten days? How else can I account for the change in her?

It was a blow to all of us; the integrity of the gang had been defeated, our luck was broken.

In the morning, Alec Gorman, defying the spotters, went down to the hospital to have a last look at him. In the evening I braved it. But I have a horror of violent death, and after one glance at him I closed my eyes and knelt down. A hand touched my shoulder.

"Dermod."

"Yes, Michael?"

"Come on out."

I went out with him. We strolled across St Vincent's Bridge and up Sunday's Well. Old Michael was literally shaking with excitement, and I saw that he was making a great struggle to regain control of himself before he spoke. But on Wyse's Hill he could stand it no longer and sank on to one of the wooden benches.

"'Twas I done it, Dermod," he said.

"What?" I asked.

"I seen it on his face. He was blaming me."

"Have sense, man," said I. "He was very fond of you."

"I brought him into it, didn't I?" he asked. "I brought you into it. I brought ye all into it."

"You did."

"And then I turned my back on ye. I reneged, and I left ye to fight alone. Didn't I?"

"You didn't," I replied consolingly. "We never doubted you, Michael, any of us."

"Ah, ah, ah, amn't I the old fool," he moaned, "amn't I the wicked old fool? Sure, ye were me own flesh and blood, the ones I put all me heart and courage into, that I cared for more than if ye were me own children. I should have known I was in the wrong, and that the best of me was in ye. After me seventy years and me three times in gaol I should have known it!"

I had to take him home. Already he seemed to be easier in his mind, as if he had shaken off a great burden.

VI

He was ill. Ellen said he was dying. One night I went to see him. He had grown a little beard which added a certain graciousness and dignity to his old head. To me he looked

160

quite well and lively, but he complained of asthma, and seemed to take it for granted that it was a complaint from which he would not recover.

All his rebel portraits he had called in from other parts of the house: O'Donovan Rossa, John O'Leary, Bryan Dillon, O'Neill Crowley – all looked at you from the crowded walls, and Michael lay like an old hero in his Fenian pantheon. He was not quite the same Michael. He was more difficult to please and had begun to be a drag on Ellen's patience. She complained of him to me even as she opened the door. He seemed to have turned completely against her, and saw far too much of the Drake, which was no credit to him and he with one foot in the grave; he even gave her money, and wouldn't I tell him that people were beginning to talk?

No sooner had Ellen shut the door behind her than the old man began complaining of her; the way she kept forcing him to do things he didn't want to do, and the sour face she put on whenever he had visitors. There was a little woman now, Mrs Broderick (it was difficult to recognise the Drake under that name, but Michael would never use a nickname to describe a lady). Mrs Broderick's grandson was in gaol for the cause; she had four other grandchildren, helpless little orphans, to feed and clothe; yet Ellen begrudged her the scrap of meat left over after their dinner!

I stood up strongly for Ellen, but he interrupted me impatiently. I could tell him nothing about Ellen. Hadn't he known her for thirty-five years?

"She's too conceited," he complained bitterly. "She thinks she's God Almighty because she've a little bit of knowledge, but she haven't got what's more important, she haven't got Christian charity."

"Anyway," I said, "the Drake is a vicious, dissolute, shameless old hag, and no woman with any bit of pride would like to have her in and about her house."

(As I spoke I saw her with the shawl dragged tight about her wizened face, her palm, varnished with filth, outstretched, and heard her high, cracked voice saying, "Alanna machree, fork out de dough!")

"You're too hard on her," muttered Michael. "We must have charity. Anyway, you don't know her."

"I do."

"You don't. I knew her when she was a girl. 'Twas only when she came to me a few weeks ago for the loan of a couple of shillings that I fixed her." He was silent for a while. Then he nodded to me and said "Whisper!"

He raised himself on the pillows; I bent across and lifted him while he put his mouth to my ear. He whispered hotly shamefastly for a moment.

"Oh, was she"? I asked without surprise. "And why didn't you marry her?"

He looked at me reproachfully, clucking his tongue in wonderment and deprecation. All the innate Gaelic conservatism rose up in him at the thought.

"Well, well, well, well, Dermod! Is it him, a national figure, a man the people of Cork looked up to? I'm surprised at you. She was only a servant in his house."

"That makes no difference," said I.

He glanced with awe and affection at the faded photograph on the wall.

"And it was after he came out of gaol, too," he said, as though that clinched it.

"He must have been over fifty then," I remarked casually.

"He was sixty-three," said Michael flatly.

He looked at me for a fraction of a second and guiltily lowered his eyes. Then a radiant blush covered all his long innocent face, spread to his ears, which began to glow scarlet about their bushes of white hair, and stealthily crept down the neck of his shirt. His thin hands fiddled nervously at the bedclothes. At last he could stand it no longer and turned his head, as though diverting his attention to what was going on along the roof-tops outside his window. But the deadly, tell-tale blush crept round the back of his neck and glowed furiously under his ears. Suddenly he dropped back without warning in the bed and covered himself with clothes until nothing appeared but two bright, abashed eyes and a crimson forehead. That was as much as I ever heard Michael say about what are called "the mysteries of life".

He had another row with Ellen before I left. Except the Fenian leaders, the only one of the heavenly hierarchies he was interested in was a group of Franciscan saints, chief of them, of course, St. Francis himself, but he developed a particular veneration for St. Rita of Cascia, and a prayer to her was nailed to the wall above his bed. He had been waiting for Ellen to come in from the chapel, and when he heard her step below stairs he called out to her.

"Did you get it?" he asked.

"Did I get what?" she shouted back.

"Oh, she wouldn't know!" he commented bitterly with a loud groan. " 'Tisn't to be expected she'd know."

She grumbled her way up the stairs and peered in.

"They hadn't it at St. Peter and Paul's."

"Did you look?"

"I told you they wouldn't have it before I went out."

" 'Tis a good job I don't want much done for me in this house."

"What is it, Michael?" I asked soothingly.

" 'Tis a life of St. Rita I'm asking that wan to get for me for a month past, but she's too lazy to stir hand or foot."

"Whatever took your fancy in St. Rita, Mr. Callanan. . . ."

There was danger in Ellen's calm tones. Her map of the heavens I knew to be carefully plotted, and she prided herself upon having tested by experiment the position of every major luminary. She had a table laden with cheap coloured statuary, and by the position of these you could at any time deduce where her speculations were tending. When a lamp was lit before a saint you might be certain that that saint was in high favour with her, and the apotheosis of her disillusionment was expressed when she turned him, face to the wall, as a punishment for his inaction. In this there was more traditional catholicism than you might imagine, for there is an Irish poem in which a saint is bitterly reproached for having withheld his favours; but Ellen did not need to rely on precedent, she was the law and the fathers in herself.

"What's that you're saying?" growled Michael.

"Whatever took your fancy in St. Rita. . . . In my humble opinion St. Rita is an Ould Show!"

"Get out," he spluttered. "Listen to her, Dermod, that's the way she's at me until she drives me past patience. I tould you before not to be irreverent."

"Oh, I'm not being irreverent, Mr. Callanan. Far from it. I'm merely expressing an opinion, which I'm perfectly entitled to do, here, or elsewhere, or at any time. I don't say that St. Rita isn't all the Church says she is. I merely say that in my opinion she's an Ould Show. Any little intention I ever asked of her was never granted, and that doesn't surprise me, Mr. Callanan, seeing who she was. I have no use for married women in religion. A woman that can't make up her mind——"

"Why shouldn't she be married?" he shouted.

"A woman that can't make up her mind," she went on imperturbably, "to leave the world *before* she takes a husband should not leave it at all."

Old Michael grew almost purple with anger.

"Are you contradicting me again?" he shouted. "Did I ask you before not to speak about St. Rita in my presence? Did I?"

"I'm sure——" she began; then she caught sight of my clenched fist being shaken at her behind the Patriarch's head. She stumbled in her speech, stuttered, came out with, "I'm sorry, I'll say no more," and left us.

There was a spring flood on the river and a high March wind when she sent for me again to say that the old man was dying. I saw by her eyes that she had been weeping. She had been up all night with him, and though he was a little better now, the doctor did not think he would last another night.

When I entered the room I saw how far gone he really

164

was. Only his eyes were alive, death had already taken the rest of him. And the magnificent spring storm was whistling and clanging along the slates and irons of the roofs outside, and the clouds, "the grey castles", that precede rain were sailing by high overhead, for long minutes plunging a whole street into gloom and chilling the white shiny face of Shandon. A great purple cloud was rising at the other side of the river; it was night coming on.

His voice was feeble, that was the "asthma" he said; it made it very difficult for him to breathe. It was about his money he wanted to speak to me. Would I take charge of it? Half his little fortune he was leaving to the Cause and half to Ellen.

"That wan," he gasped faintly, "she'd disgust you, she'd positively disgust you! She's crossing and thwarting that poor Mrs. Broderick, all because she's in dread I'd leave her me money."

"She's a good, pious woman," I said, "so let her alone."

"Good?" He clucked his tongue at me, in pity for my wits. "Good? When I was gasping me last in this bed during the night, did she say that prayer to St. Rita? Did she? To St. Rita of Cascia, the Patroness of the Impossible? Did she? She did not." His disgust went beyond all bounds. "That wan, Dermod, whisper to me, she was praying for hours, and do you know? She was *making up* saints."

It was all so strange: here was death— here the hero of my boyhood, and I was listening only to a display of senile hatred of his housekeeper. Strange, I thought, how death tries to divest itself of all human dignity!

I heard the Drake sigh as she came in below stairs.

"Mercy, mercy, mercy!" she panted, trying to force the shop door to behind her. " 'Twould tear you into tatters, dat wind!"

Ellen and she came up. It was darkening to an early nightfall. The old man would not have the lamp lit, so she put a match to the candle on the dresser.

"Dat wind," said the Drake, "would shake you asunder. Mike Callanan, you're a lucky man to be lying dere in your warm comfortable bed instead of being out under dat like me."

"Where were you?' he asked feebly.

"Where was I? I was foraging, what else?" She laughed her high, cracked laugh. "I was foraging. Bridie is going to make her confirmation, if you please, and dey wanted me to get a dress for her. Where did dey tink I was going to get the money for a dress for her? So I wint up to Fader Duane. 'Dis and dat,' says I, 'the teacher wants a new dress for Bridie for her confirmation, and, God help me,' says I, 'where would I get the price of a new dress?' So he put his hand in his pocket and what do you tink he gives me, my dear? What do you tink?"

"I dunno," says Michael.

"He give me half-a-crown. How did he tink I'd buy a dress for a half-a-crown? And I ups and tells him so, my dear, so I did! 'Dat's all you're going to get from me, y'oul vagabone,' says he. 'If dat's the way it is, fader,' says I, 'if dat's the way it is, I won't be troubling you,' says I, 'but I'll go down to Minister Bolster and see if he won't give it to me.'" She laughed again. "Off I wint, my dear, off I wint, and Fader Duane after me, and I starts running and he starts running. 'Come back,' says he. O, he chased me down Shandon Street I declare, before Jesus and the world!"

The wind is blowing more loudly, tugging with might and main at the windows. Rain has begun to fall heavily. The candle flickers; the old hag gets into a violent discussion about religion with Ellen.

"Nuns? Nuns?" I hear her exclaim. "Dey'd work you to train oil for a half-a-crown!"

"Dermod," says old Michael faintly, and I go and sit by him.

"This night," he said. "It reminds me of when I was a boy. There's a flood on the river, you said?"

"There is."

"It was when I was six or seven. We were evicted from the little house in Dunmanway. Can you hear me?"

"Yes."

"We had to come into the city and take a room for the three of us, my grandmother, my mother and myself. 'Tis funny I didn't think of it until tonight. There was an old man staying with us in Dunmanway, but he wouldn't come in here at all. He hung round the old wreck of a house after the soldiers and baliffs were done with it. For four months. Until the winter came on."

"Go on."

"Then he got lonely and downhearted. He wanted to come in to us, but he didn't know how to find us. He couldn't speak English, you see. He started to walk the thirty odd miles. He was so old it took him three days. He got here one night after dark. The river was in a flood, and the rain was falling, and the wind was up, just like now. He asked the few people he met for the Callanans, but none of them had heard of us, natural enough. The water was up to his knees and the wind was pelting him. And then what did he do? He went from street to street, crying out in his Irish, and what do you think he called?"

"I don't know. I suppose he called for you."

"He called − in Irish that was − his curse on God (his voice dropped to the faintest of whispers) for sending the floods and the wind, and God's curse on the Callanans for losing their land."

"And ye heard him?"

"My grandmother heard him. She was blind, and she could hear what you were thinking almost. She cocked her head, and she said 'That is the voice of Donal the Piper O'Leary!' and my mother went downstairs and brought him in, nearly dying. He was after being two hours calling then. He lived with us for six years after. . . ."

The two women had gone downstairs. When I went down to call Ellen to him, the old hag and she were still fighting.

"When you're dead," said Ellen, "your soul flies like a bird to the judgment seat of God!"

"When you're dead," said the Drake, spitting on the

167

floor, "you go down into the eart, and neider Fader Duane nor Minister Bolster can put a stir in your little finger or your big toe."

It was about two o'clock when old Michael died. For an hour before a sniper had been at work, and when the wind blew towards us the shot would ring out, as though it were being fired in the room, and then we would hear everything off stage, the sniper's rifle and the rattle of a machine gun. Michael lay in a heavy stupor. At last he came to with a start; his breathing became more and more laboured, his face turned purple, and before I could reach him he leaped out of bed. I caught him in my arms, but he gasped and struggled fiercely, his lips growing darker, his tongue protruding. Then he shook me off and reached the window. He forced it up, and fell upon the sill, his two hands clutching at his throat. I bent over him and heard the death rattle there. Ellen was on her knees saying the "De Profundis" when the candle went out in the high, raging wind. She continued, however, and the darkness was filled with the noise of the storm, the spluttering of the rain about the floor, the cracking of the sniper's rifle – all magnified into something terrifying, remote, and cruel – and her frightened, penetrating voice that made the last supplications.

"If thou shalt mark iniquities, Lord, who shall endure it?"

After Fourteen Years

Nicholas Coleman arrived in Bantry on a fair day. The narrow streets were crowded with cattle that lurched and lounged dangerously as the drovers goaded them out of the way of passing cars. The air was charged with smells and dust and noise. Jobbers swung their sticks and shouted at one another across the street; shopkeepers displayed their wares and haggled with customers on the high pavements; shrill-voiced women sold apples, cigarettes and lemonade about the statue of the Maid of Erin in the market-place, and jovial burly farmers with shrewd ascetic faces under their Spanish hats jostled him as they passed.

He was glad when he succeeded in getting his business done and could leave the town for a while. It unnerved him. Above the roofs one could see always the clear grey-green of a hill that rose sharply above them and seemed as if at any moment it might fall and crush them. The sea road was better. There were carts on that too, and creels passed full of squealing animals; but at least one had the great bay with its many islands and its zone of violet hills through which sunlight and shadow circulated ceaselessly, without effort, like the flowing of water. The surface of the bay was very calm, and it seemed as if a rain of sunlight were pelting upon a bright flagstone and being tossed back again in a faint glittering spray, so that when one looked at it for long it dazzled the eye. Three or four fishing smacks and a little railway steamer with a bright red funnel were all that the bay held.

He had his dinner over an old shop in the market-place, but he was so nervous that he ate little. The farmers and jobbers tried to press him into conversation, but he had nothing to say; they talked of prices and crops, the Government and the County Council, about all of which he knew next to nothing. Eventually they let him be, much to his relief.

After dinner he climbed the hill that led out of town. The traffic had grown less: he climbed, and as the town sank back against the growing circle of the bay it seemed a quiet place enough, too quiet perhaps. He felt something like awe as he went up the trim gravel path of the convent. "At seven," he thought, "the train will take me back to the city. At ten I shall be walking through Patrick Street on my way home. Tomorrow I shall be back at my old stool in the office, I shall never see this place again, never!"

But in spite of this, and partly because of it, his heart beat faster when the lay sister showed him into the bare parlour, with its crucifix, its polished floor, its wide-open windows that let in a current of cool air.

And at last *she* came; a slim figure in black with starched white facings. He scarcely looked at her, but took her hand, smiling, embarrassed and silent. She too was ill at ease.

They sat together on a garden seat from which he saw again the town and the bay, even more quiet now. He heard nothing of its noise but the desolate screech of a train as it entered the station. Her eyes took it all in dispassionately, and now and again he glanced shyly up at her fine profile. That had not changed, and he wondered whether he had altered as little as she. Perhaps he hadn't, perhaps for her at least he was still the same as he had always been. Yet — there was a change in her! Her face had lost something; perhaps it was intensity; it no longer suggested the wildness and tenderness that he knew was in her. She looked happier and stronger.

"And Kate?" she asked after they had talked for a little while. "How is she?"

"Oh, Kate is very well. They have a nice house in Passage — you know Tom has a school there. It's just over the river – the house, I mean; sometimes I go down to them on a Sunday evening for tea. . . . They have five children now; the eldest is sixteen."

"Yes, of course – Marie. Why, she was called after me! She's my godchild."

"Yes, yes, fancy I'd forgotten! You were always with Kate in those days."

"I'd love to see Marie. She has written to me for my feastday ever since she was nine."

"Has she? I didn't know. They don't talk to me about it."

A faint flush mounted her cheek; for a moment she was silent, and if he had looked at her he would have seen a sudden look of doubt and pain in her eyes. But he did not look up, and she continued.

"Kate writes to me off and on too – but you know Kate! It was from her I heard of your mother's death. That must have been a terrible blow to you."

"Yes, it was very sudden. I was the only one with her when it came."

"We had Mass for her here. How did she die? Was she——?"

"She died hard. She didn't want to leave me."

"Oh!"

Her lips moved silently for a little.

"I've never forgotten her. She was so gentle, so – so unobtrusive, and Fair Hill used to be such a happy place then, before Kate married, when there were only the three of ourselves. . . . Do you remember, I used to go without my dinner to come up after school? . . . And so the house is gone?"

"Yes, the house is gone."

"And Jennifer? The parrot?"

"Jennifer died long ago. She choked herself with an apple."

"And Jasper?"

"Jasper too. An Alsatian killed him. I have another now, a sheepdog, a great lazy fellow. He's made friends with the

Kerry Blue next door and the Kerry Blue comes with us and catches rabbits for him. He's fond of rabbits, but he's so big, so big and lazy!"

"You're in lodgings. Why didn't you go to live with Kate and Tom? You know they'd have been glad to have you."

"Why should I? They were married; they had children at the time; they needed the house for themselves. . . . Besides, you know what I am. I'm a simple fellow, I'm not a bit clever, I don't read books or papers. At dinner the cattle-jobbers were trying to get me talking politics, and honest, I didn't know what they were at! What would Tom and his friends from the University have thought of a stupid creature like me?"

"No, you spent all your time in the country. I remember you getting up at five and going out with the dogs around White's Cross and back through Ballyvolane. Do you still do that?"

"Yes, every fine morning and most Sundays. But I had to give up the birds when mother died."

"Ah, the birds! What a pity! I remember them too, and how beautifully they sang." She laughed happily, without constraint. "The other girls envied me so much because you were always giving me birds' eggs, and I swapped them for other things, and I came back to you crying, pretending I'd lost them. . . . I don't think you ever guessed what a cheat I was. . . . Ah, well! And you're still in the factory."

"Still in the factory! . . . You were right, you see. Do you remember you said I'd stick there until I grew grey hairs. You used to be angry with me then, and that worried me, and I'd give a spurt or two – No, no, I never had any ambition – not much anyhow – and as well be there as any place else. . . . And now I'm so used to it that I couldn't leave even if I wanted to. I live so quietly that even coming here has been too much of an adventure for me. All the time I've been saying 'Tomorrow I shall be back at work, tomorrow I shall be back at work.' I'll be glad to get home."

"Yes, I can understand that."

"Can you? You used to be different."

"Yes, but things *are* different here. One works. One doesn't think. One doesn't want to think. I used to lie abed until ten at one time, now I'm up at half-past five every morning and I'm not a bit more tired. I'm kept busy all day. I sleep sound. I don't dream. And I hate anything that comes to disturb the routine."

"Like me?"

"No, not like you. I hate being ill, lying in bed listening to the others and not working myself."

"And you don't get into panics any longer?"

"No, no more panics."

"You don't weep? You're not ambitious any longer? — that's so strange! . . . Yes, it *is* good to have one's life settled, to fear nothing and hope for nothing."

She cast a quick, puzzled look at him.

"Do you still go to early Mass?" she asked.

"Yes, just as before."

They fell into silence again. A little mist was rising from the town; one side of the bay was flanked with a wall of gold; a cool wind from the sea blew up to them, stirring the thick foliage and tossing her light, black veil. A bell rang out suddenly and she rose.

"What are your lodgings like?" she asked, her cheeks reddening. "I hope you look after yourself and that they feed you properly. You used to be so careless."

"Oh, yes, yes. They're very decent. And you — how do you find the place agreeing with you? Better than the city?"

"Oh, of course," she said wearily, "it is milder here."

They went silently up the path towards the convent and parted as they had met, awkwardly, almost without looking at one another.

"No," he thought, as he passed through the convent gate, "that's over!" But he knew that for days, perhaps for months, birds and dogs, flowers, his early-morning walks through the country, the trees in summer, all those things that had given him pleasure would give him nothing but pain. The farmers coming from the fair, shouting to one another forward and back from their lumbering carts brought to mind his dreams of yesterday, and he grieved that God had created men without the innocence of natural things, had created them subtle and capricious, with memories in which the past existed like a statue, perfect and unapproachable.

And as the train carried him back to the city the clangour of its wheels that said "ruthutta ruthutta ruthutta" dissolved into a bright mist of conversation through which he distinctly heard a woman's voice, but the voice said nothing; it was like memory, perfect and unapproachable; and his mind was weighed down by an infinite melancholy that merged with the melancholy of the dark countryside through which he passed – a countryside of lonely, steelbright pools that were islanded among the silhouettes of hills and trees. Ironically he heard himself say again, "Yes, it *is* good to have one's life settled, to fear nothing and hope for nothing."

And the train took him ever farther and farther away and replied with its petulant metallic voice— "Ruthutta ruthutta ruthutta!"

The Late Henry Conran

"I've another little story for you," said the old man.

"I hope it's a good one," said I.

"The divil a better. And if you don't believe me you can go down to Courtenay's Road and see the truth of it with your own two eyes. Now it isn't every wan will say that to you?"

"It is not then."

"And the reason I say it is, I know the people I'm talking about. I knew Henry in the old days – Henry Conran that is, otherwise known as 'Prosperity' Conran – and I'll say for him he had the biggest appetite for liquor of any man I ever met or heard of. You could honestly say 'Prosperity' Conran would drink porter out of a sore heel. Six foot three he was, and he filled it all. He was quiet enough when he was sober, but when he was drunk – Almighty and Eternal, you never knew what divilment he'd be up to!

"I remember calling for him wan night to go to a comity meeting – he was a great supporter of John Redmond – and finding him mad drunk, in his shirt and drawers; he was trying to change out of his old working clothes. Well, with respects to you, he got sick on it, and what did he do before me own two eyes but strip off every stitch he had on him and start wiping up the floor with his Sunday clothes. Oh, every article he could find he shoved into it. And there he was idioty drunk in his pelt singing

> Up the Mollies! Hurray!
> We don't care about Quarry Lane,
> All we want is our own Fair Lane.

"Well, of course, poor Henry couldn't keep any job, and his own sweet Nellie wasn't much help to him. She was a nagging sort of woman, if you understand me, an unnatural sort of woman. She had six children to rear, and, instead of going quietly to work and softening Henry, she was always calling in the priest or the minister to him. And Henry, to get his own back, would smash every bit of china she had. Not that he was a cross man by any manner of means, but he was a bit independent, and she could never see how it slighted him to call in strangers like that.

"Henry hung round idle for six months. Then he was offered a job to go round the town as a walking advertisement for somebody's ale. That cut him to the heart. As he said himself, 'Is it me, a comity man of the Ancient Order of Hibernians, a man dat shook hands with John Dillon, to disgrace meself like dat before the town? And you wouldn't mind but I couldn't as much as stomach the same hogwash meself!'

"So he had to go to America, and sorry I was to lose him, the decent man! Nellie told me after 'twould go through you to see him on the deck of the tender, blue all over and smothered with sobs. 'Nellie,' says he to her, 'Nellie, give the word and I'll trow me ticket in the water.' 'I will not', says Nellie, 'for you were always a bad head to me.'

"Now that was a hard saying, and maybe it wasn't long before she regretted it. There she was with her six children, and wan room between the seven of them, and she trying to do a bit of laundry to keep the life in their bodies.

"Well, it would be a troublesome thing for me to relate all that happened them in the twenty-five long years between that day and this. But maybe you'd remember how her son, Aloysius, mixed himself up in the troubles? Maybe you would? Not that he ever did anything dangerous except act as clerk of the court, and be on all sorts of relief comities, and go here and go there on delegations and deputations. No shooting or jailing for Aloysius.

'Lave that,' says he, 'to the rank and file!' All he ever had his eye on was the main chance. And grander and grander he was getting in himself, my dear! First he had to buy out the house, then he had an electric bell put in, then he bought or hobbled a motor car, then he found tidy jobs for two of his sisters and one for his young brother. Pity to God the two big girls were married already or he'd have made a rare haul! But God help them, they were tied to two poor boozy sops that weren't half nor quarter the cut of their father! So Aloysius gave them the cold shoulder.

"Now Nellie wasn't liking this at all in her own mind. She often said to me, 'For all me grandeur, I'd be better off with poor Henry,' and so she would, for about that time Aloysius began to think of choosing a wife. Of course, the wife-to-be was a flashy piece from the country, and Nellie, who didn't like her at all, was for ever crossing her and finding fault with her. Sure, you ought to remember the row she kicked up when the damsel appeared wan night in wan of them new-fangled sleeping things with trousers. Nellie was so shocked she went to the priest and complained her, and then complained her to all the neighbours, and she shamed and disgraced Aloysius so much that for months he wouldn't speak to her. But begod, if she didn't make that girl wear a plain shift every other time she came to stay with them!

"After the scandal about the trousers nothing would content Aloysius but that they must live away from the locality, so they got another house, a bigger wan this time, and it was from the new house that Aloysius got married. Nellie, poor woman, couldn't read nor write, so she had nothing at all to do with the preparations, and what was her surprise when the neighbours read out the marriage announcement to her! 'Aloysius Gonzaga Conran, son of Ellen Conran, Courtenay's Road' — and divil the word about poor Henry! The whole town was laughing at it, but what annoyed Nellie most was not the slight on herself, but the slight on her man. So up with her to Aloysius, and 'this and that', she says, 'I didn't pick you up from under a bush, so give your father the bit of credit that's due to him or I'll put in the note meself!' My dear, she was foaming! Aloysius was in a cleft stick, and they fought and fought, Aloysius calling his father down, and Nellie praising him, and then the young wife drops the suggestion that they should put in 'the Late Henry Conran'. So Nellie not having a word to say against that, next day there is another announcement – nothing about Nellie this time only plain 'son of the late Henry Conran.'

"Well, the town is roaring yet! Wan day the man have no father to speak of and the next day he have a dead father and no mother at all. And everybody knowing at the same time that Henry was in America, safe and sound, and wilder that ever he was at home.

"But that's not the end of it. I was in me bed the other night when a knock came to the door. My daughter-in-law opened it and I heard a strange voice asking for me. Blast me if I could place it! And all at once the stranger forces his way in apast her and stands in the bedroom door, with his head bent down and wan hand on the jamb. 'Up the Mollies!' says he in the top of his voice. 'Me ould flower, strike up the antem of Fair Lane! Do you remember the night we carried deat and destruction into Blackpool? Shout it, me hearty man – Up the Mollies!'

"But 'twas the height I recognised.

" ' 'Tis Prosperity Conran,' says I.

" 'Prosperity Conran it is,' says he.

" 'The same ould six foot three?' says I.

" 'Every inch of it!' says he, idioty drunk.

" 'And what in the name of God have you here?' says I.

" 'Me wife dat put a notice in the papers saying I was dead. Am I dead, Larry Costello? Me lovely man, you knew me since I was tree – tell me if I'm dead. Feel me! Feel dat muscle of mine and tell me the trute, am I alive or dead?'

" 'You're not dead,' says I after I felt his arm.

" 'I'll murder her, dat's what I'll do! I'll smash every bone in her body. Get up now, Larry, and I'll show you

178

the greatest bust up dat was ever seen or heard of in dis city. Where's the All-For-Ireland Headquarters till I fling a brick at it?'

" 'The All-For-Irelands is no more,' says I.

"He looked at me unsteadily for a minute.

" 'Joking me you are,' says he.

" 'Divil a joke,' says I.

" 'The All-For-Irelands gone?'

" 'All gone,' says I.

" 'And the Mollies?'

" 'All gone.'

" 'All gone?'

" 'All gone.'

" 'Dat you might be killed?'

" 'That I might be killed stone dead.'

" 'Merciful God! I must be an ould man then, huh?'

" ' 'Tisn't younger we're getting,' says I.

" 'An ould man,' says he, puzzled-like. 'Maybe I'm dead after all? Do you think I'm dead, Larry?'

" 'In a manner of speaking you are,' says I.

" 'Would a court say I was dead?'

" 'A clever lawyer might argue them into it,' says I.

" 'But not *dead*, Larry? Christ, he couldn't say I was *dead*?'

" 'Well, as good as dead, Henry.'

" 'I'll carry the case to the High Courts,' says he getting excited. 'I'll prove I'm not dead. I'm an American citizen and I can't be dead.'

" 'Aisy! Aisy!' says I, seeing him take it so much to heart.

" 'I won't be aisy,' says he, flaring up. 'I've a summons out agin me wife for defaming me character, and I'll never go back to Chicago till I clear me name in the eyes of the world.'

" 'Henry,' says I, 'no wan ever said wan word against you. There isn't as much as a shadow of an aspersion on your character.'

" 'Do you mane,' says he, ' 'tis no aspersion on me

character to say I'm dead? God damn you, man, would you like a rumour like dat to be going round about yourself?'

" 'I would not, Henry, I would not, but 'tis no crime to be dead. And anyway, as I said before, 'tis only a manner of speaking. A man might be stone dead, or he might be half dead, or dead to you and me, or, for the matter of that, he might be dead to God and the world as we've often been ourselves.'

" 'Dere's no manner of speaking in it at all,' says Henry, getting madder and madder. 'No bloody manner of speaking. I might be dead drunk as you say, but dat would be no excuse for calling me the late Henry Conran. . . . Dere's me charge sheet,' says he, sitting on the bed and pulling out a big blue paper. 'Ellen Conran, for defamation of character. Wan man on the boat wanted me to charge her with attempted bigamy, but the clerk wouldn't have it.'

" 'And did you come all the way from America to do this?' says I.

" 'Of course I did. How could I stay on in America wit a ting like dat hanging over me? Blast you, man, you don't seem to know the agony I went trough for weeks and weeks before I got on the boat!'

" 'And do Nellie know you're here?' says I.

" 'She do not, and I mane her not to know it till the policeman serves his warrant on her.'

" 'Listen to me, Henry,' says I getting out of bed, 'the sooner you have this out with Nellie the better for all.'

" 'Do you tink so?' says he a bit stupid-like.

" 'How long is it since you put your foot aboard the liner in Queenstown, Henry?'

" ' 'Tis twenty-five years and more,' says he.

" ' 'Tis a long time not to see your own lawful wife,' says I.

" ' 'Tis,' says he, ' 'tis, a long time,' and all at wance he began to cry, with his head in his two hands.

" 'I knew she was a hard woman, Larry, but blast me if I ever tought she'd do the like of dat on me! Me poor ould heart is broke! And the Mollies – did I hear you say the Mollies was gone?'

" 'The Mollies is gone,' says I.

" 'Anyting else but dat, Larry, anyting else but dat!'

" 'Come on away,' says I.

"So I brought him down the road by the hand just like a child. He never said wan word till I knocked at the door, and all at wance he got fractious again. I whispered into Nellie to open the door. When she seen the man with me she nearly went through the ground.

" 'Who is it?' says she.

" 'An old friend of yours,' says I.

" 'Is it Henry?' says she, whispering-like.

" 'It is Henry,' says I.

" 'It is not Henry!' bawls out me hero. 'Well you know your poor ould Henry is dead and buried without a soul in the world to shed a tear over his corpse.'

" 'Henry!' says she.

" 'No, blast you!' says he with a shriek, 'but Henry's ghost come to ha'ant you.'

" 'Come in, come in the pair of ye,' says I. 'Why the blazes don't ye kiss wan another like any Christian couple?'

"After a bit of trouble I dragged him inside.

" 'Ah, you hard-hearted woman!' says he moaning, with his two paws out before him like a departed spirit. 'Ah, you cruel, wicked woman! What did you do to your poor ould husband?'

" 'Help me to undress him, Nellie,' says I. 'Sit down there on the bed, Henry, and let me unlace your boots.'

"So I pushed him back on the bed, but, when I tried to get at his boots, he began to kick his feet up in the air, laughing like a kid.

" 'I'm dead, dead, dead, dead,' says he.

" 'Let me get at him, Larry,' says Nellie in her own determined way, so, begod, she lifted his legs that high he couldn't kick without falling over, and in two minits she had his boots and stockings off. Then I got off his coat, loosened his braces and held him back in the bed while she pulled his trousers down. At that he began to come to himself a bit.

" 'Show it to her! Show it to her!' says he, getting hot and making a dive for his clothes.

" 'Show what to her?' says I.

" 'Me charge sheet. Give it to me, Larry. There you are, you jade of hell! Seven and sixpence I paid for it to clear me character.'

" 'Get into bed, sobersides,' says I.

" 'I wo' not go into bed!'

" 'And there's an old nightshirt all ready,' says Nellie.

" 'I don't want no nightshirt. I'll take no charity from any wan of ye. I wants me character back, me character that ye took on me.'

" 'Take off his shirt, Larry,' says she.

"So I pulled the old stinking shirt up over his grey pate, and in a tick of the clock she had his nightshirt on.

" 'Now, Nellie,' says I, 'I'll be going. There's nothing more I can do for you.'

" 'Thanks, Larry, thanks,' says she. 'You're the best friend we ever had. There's nothing else you can do. He'll be asleep in a minit, don't I know him well?'

" 'Good-night, Henry,' says I.

" 'Good-night, Larry. Tomorrow we'll revive the Mollies.'

"Nellie went to see me to the door, and outside was the two ladies and the young gentleman in their nighties, listening.

" 'Who is it, mother?' says they.

" 'Go back to bed the three of ye!' says Nellie. ' 'Tis only your father.'

" 'Jesus, Mary and Joseph!' says the three of them together.

"At that minit we heard Henry inside bawling his heart out.

" 'Nellie, Nellie, where are you, Nellie?'

" 'Go back and see what he wants,' says I, 'before I go.'

"So Nellie opened the door and looked in.

" 'What's wrong with you now?' says she.

" 'You're not going to leave me sleep alone, Nellie,' says he.

" 'You ought to be ashamed of yourself,' says she, 'talking like that and the children listening. . . . Look at him,' says she to me, 'look at him for the love of God!' The eyes were shining in her head with pure relief. So I peeped in, and there was Henry with every bit of clothes in the bed around him and his back to us all. 'Look at his ould grey pate!' says she.

" 'Still in all,' says Henry over his shoulder, 'you had no right to say I was dead!' "

The Sisters

It was Norah Coveney, who has more queer stories than anyone in Cork, who told me this one, and I have tried to retell it, so far as I could, in her own words.

Miss Kate and Miss Ellen — God rest them both, the creatures! — came to live in Blarney Lane, oh, long years ago now! but where they came from or who they were we didn't know at the time. Miss Kate opened a little shop, and for two years it flourished in her care alone. No one ever saw Miss Ellen, though we were always speaking of her, or if we weren't Miss Kate was quick to remind us, for 'twas as if she had that poor sister of hers on the brain. "And how's yourself?" you'd ask by way of being neighbourly, and pat as tuppence she'd say, "Finely, thank God, I'm finely, but Miss Ellen isn't herself at all these times," or, as might be, "Miss Ellen is very quiet in herself, thanks be to you, God!" So it came about that her poor mad sister was as much in our minds as Miss Kate herself — or more maybe — and we'd ask about her as you'd ask about one you'd known since you were a child growing up beside her.

'Twas how we understood it: there was this strain in the family, and Miss Kate being too proud to have her sister locked up on her, kept her and fed her and minded her, as any of us would like to do for our own. And when I say Miss Kate was proud I mean it, my dear! Though she'd talk to you at the counter as well as another, never would she invite you inside to have a cup of tea or a look at the house. Nor was she ever known to smile, but always discreet and managing; a near, tight, slim, shabby little woman with two hard lips, you'd see her off to do her shopping when the men were going to work, and on the stroke of ten she'd close her little shutters, and up the stairs with her to bed. Often and often when I passed and seen that light burning in the upstairs room I thought to myself, my dear, the life that poor woman must lead, trying to control her sister that was so often outrageous, as she gave you to understand. And that, as we all thought, excusing her sharpness and her being a little bit queer, was the greatest burden the Lord could lay on her.

Well, one morning we seen the shutters up till noon and no sign of Miss Kate, but like that in the story none of us wanted to be first in, for though a neighbour's a neighbour no one would care to intrude where she wasn't wanted. But as evening drew near, and the house looked just as quiet as before, some of us made so bold as to knock, and there being no reply, one of the men forced the door for us. And when we stole in, my dear, there was Miss Kate, sitting all alone by the fireplace, fully dressed, but never to see the light again. It was a shock, I tell you, I never forgot! There wasn't a hair astray on her to tell you what happened, and she as cold and waxy as a three-days' corpse. We sent the men off, some to the priest and some to the police, and Bridgie Flynn crept upstairs on tiptoe to see what was there. Miss Kate's door, as she explained it, was wide open, and what should she see on the dresser, my dear, but a new blue shroud! As I said then, even death couldn't take that poor creature by surprise.

Well, a doctor came and told us – what we knew already – that she was dead overnight; a policeman – it was Bill Conboy, by the same token – came and wrote down our names and all we had to say about the deceased, and a message came saying the priest would drop in later to arrange about the funeral. Then Minnie came in, Minnie Mac, the market woman, and she clapped her two hands on her hips and asked us in the name of Almighty God what were we doing there all night and had we no respect for the dead.

Within five minutes Minnie had the place cleared of

men (including old Conboy), and with her own two hands she stripped the corpse and lifted it on the table to wash it. She sent me out to get my own two brass candlesticks and borrow two more, and by the time we left old Conboy in, she was after arranging a lovely wake. There on the table with her flowers and rosary beads and candles lay Miss Kate and the last wrinkle long faded from her poor old face.

So we set to under Minnie's orders and made a cup of tea for old Conboy who was to face upstairs before he was relieved, to see what could be done with the poor mad woman, and Minnie and himself started swapping yarns about all the queer deaths they had ever seen or heard of when suddenly – as true as God I nearly died – the door opened in on us, and there was the queerest little creature you ever seen, in a white nightdress with white hair sticking out all over her head.

"Almighty and Merciful!" whispers Bridgie Flynn to me, " 'tis the mad sister!"

So there we sat stupefied, the lot of us, and the little creature without as much as pushing the door in one inch more, started making queer sounds, passing her tongue over her lips every now and again as if she was moistening them. And it was another minute or so before we could even make out what she was saying – oh, a weeshy, scared, cracked, little voice she had, like a sparrow.

"Am I made welcome, neighbours?" that was what she said. "Am I made welcome?"

Minnie Mac, as you'd expect, was the first to make a move, though God knows she looked frightened enough. She rose from her stool, pulling the old shawl tight about her shoulders.

"What's that you say, ma'am?" she says politely, just as if she was looking for a fight.

The little woman behind the door moistened her lips again and again.

"Am I made welcome?" she says at last, as if it was a trial to her to say it.

186

Well, I noticed Minnie Mac looking at her in a queer sort of puzzled way, up and down and back again. Then she gave one yell out of her that was like a sergeant of the guard calling his men to order. I never before nor since heard such a ring in any woman's voice, and the two eyes were standing in her head.

"Move up there, women!" she bawled. "Move up, I tell ye! Come in, ma'am, come in!" she says, grabbing the little woman by the two shoulders and flinging her own shawl around her. "Bridgie Flynn, hot up the kettle, hot it up this instant! The poor soul must be famished!"

So, begob, Minnie planked Miss Ellen down beside her at the fire, and pulled her feet up on the fender, and covered her round and round with the shawl, and by the way she talked you'd think 'twas a stray child of her own she had. And none of us said one word, but old Conboy pulled out his big notebook, and then, catching a wink from Minnie, put it back again. At last, Bridgie Flynn, that great gom — I never forgave her for it — filled out the cup of tea and handed it to Miss Ellen.

"Take the tay, poor woman," says she with her idioty smile. "You've no wan now to mind you but Almighty God!"

At that minute Minnie's eye caught her one melting, withering look that was as good as a summons.

"Who do she want to mind her, you fool?" said she, and there was a fright of bitterness in the way she said it. "Who do she want to mind her, will you tell me? Is it that poor creature on the table?"

I tell you there was a silence like the grave in that room for a full minute, an awful silence, and we looked at the corpse and back at Minnie, and at long last light began to dawn on us one by one. We were stupefied, that's what we were, stupefied! And I remember as this day how we heard Shandon strike through the window, and how clear it sounded, and all at once the poor woman sitting at the fire began to sob her heart out, and Minnie said again and again "There, there, there, the creature!" and pulling out

187

an old comb began to run it through Miss Ellen's white hair.

"And is that all the story?" I asked when Norah Coveney had finished. She was looking away from me, as though seeing it all again.

"What more do you want?" she asked roughly.

"And it was the other woman – Miss Kate——?"

"Of course it was Miss Kate! Amn't I telling you?"

"And what happened Miss Ellen after?"

"You might ask your mother that. Many's the cup of tea herself and me and Minnie Mac drank in Miss Ellen's back parlour."

"And you never asked her how it all came about?"

" 'Tis the sort of thing you'd do yourself I suppose?" asked Norah pertly.

"I suppose I wouldn't," I admitted unwillingly.

"My oath on it you wouldn't!" said Norah with conviction.

The Procession of Life

At last his father had fulfilled his threat. He was locked out. Since his mother died, a year ago, it had been a cause of dire penalties and direr threats, this question of hours. "Early to bed," his father quoted, insisting that he should be home by ten o'clock. He, a grown boy of sixteen to be home at ten o'clock like any kid of twelve! He had risked being late a dozen times before, but tonight had cooked it properly. There was the door locked against him, not a light in the house, and a stony ear to all his knockings and whisperings.

By turns he felt miserable and elated. He had tried sleeping in a garden, but that wasn't a success. Then he had wandered aimlessly into the city and been picked up by a policeman. He looked so young and helpless that the policeman wanted to take him to the barracks, but this was not included in his plans for the night. So he promised the policeman that he would go home directly, and no sooner was he out of the policeman's sight, than he doubled down the quay at the opposite side of the bridge. He walked on for at least a mile until he judged himself safe. The quays were lonely and full of shadows, and he sighed with relief when he saw a watchman's fire glowing redly on the waterfront. He went up to it, and said good-night to the watchman, who was an oldish, bearded man with a sour and repulsive face.

He sat in his little sentry-box, smoking his pipe, and looked, thought Larry, for all the world like a priest in the confessional. But he was swathed in coats and scarves, and a second glance made Larry think not of a priest but of some heathen idol; his face was so bronzed above the grey beard and glowed so majestically in the flickering light of the brasier.

Larry didn't like his situation at all, but he felt his only hope was to stick near the watchman. The city smouldering redly between its hills was in some way unfamiliar and frightening. So were the quays all round him. There were shadowy heaps of timber lying outside the range of the watchman's fire, and behind these he imagined all sorts of strange and frightening things. The river made a clucking, lonely sound against the quay wall, and three or four ships, almost entirely in darkness, swayed about close to the farther bank. He heard the noisy return of a party of sailors from across the water, and once two Lascars went past him in the direction of the bridge.

But the watchman did not seem to welcome Larry's company as much as Larry welcomed his. He was openly incredulous when Larry said he had been locked out.

"Locked out?" he asked suspiciously. "Then why didn't you kick up hell, huh?"

"What's that, sir?" asked Larry, startled.

"Why didn't you bate the door and kick up hell's delights?"

"God, sir, I'd be afraid to do that!"

At this the watchman started blindly from his box, rubbing the sleep from his eyes and swaying about in the heavy fumes of the brasier.

"Afraid?" he exclaimed scornfully. "A boy of your age to be afraid of his own father? When I was your age I wouldn't let meself be treated like that. I had a girl of me own, and the first time me ould fella' — God rest him! — tried to stop me going with her I up with the poker, and hit him such a clout over the poll they had to put six stitches in him in the Infirmary after."

Larry shuddered.

"And what did he do then, sir?" he asked innocently.

"What did he do then?" growled the watchman. "Ech, he was a quiet man after that I tell you! He couldn't look.

190

at me after in the light of day but he'd get a reeling in his head."

"Lord, sir," said Larry, "you must have hit him a terrible stroke!"

"Oh, I quietened him," said the watchman complacently. "I quietened him sure enough. . . . And there's a big fella' like you now, and you'd let your father bate you, and never rise a hand in your own self-defence?"

"I would, God help me!" said Larry.

"I suppose you never touched a drop of drink in your life?"

"I did not."

"And you never took a girl out for a walk?"

"I didn't."

"Had you ever as much as a pipe in your mouth, tell me?"

"I took a couple of pulls out of me father's pipe once," said Larry brokenly. "And I was retching until morning."

"No wonder you're locked out!" said the watchman contemptously. "No wonder at all! I think if I'd a son like you 'twould give me all I could do to keep me hands off him. Get out of me sight!"

Terrified at this extraordinary conclusion, Larry retreated to the edge of the circle of light. He dared not go farther.

"Get out of me sight!" said the watchman again.

"You won't send me away now, sir?" asked Larry in despair.

"Won't I?" asked the watchman ironically. "Won't I just? There's people comes here at every hour of the night, and am I going to have it said I gathered all the young blackguards of the city about me?"

"I'd go mad with lonesomeness," Larry cried, his voice rising on a note of fear.

"You'll find company enough in the tramp's shelter on the Marina."

"I won't go, I won't go! I'll dodge behind the timbers if a stranger comes."

"You'll do nothing of the kind," the watchman shouted, losing his temper. "Clear out now and don't let me see your ugly mug again."

"I won't go!" Larry repeated hysterically, evading him by running round the brasier. "I'm frightened, I tell you."

He had plainly heard the sound of quick footsteps coming in his direction, and he was determined that he would stay. The watchman, too, had heard them, and was equally determined that he would go.

"Bad luck to you!" he whispered despairingly, "what misfortune brought you this way tonight. If you don't go away I'll strangle you and drop your naked body in the river for the fish to ate. Be off with you, you devil's brat!"

He succeeded in chasing Larry for a few yards when the footsteps suddenly stopped and a woman's voice called out:

"Anybody there?"

"I am," said the watchman, surlily abandoning the chase.

"I thought you were lost," the woman said, and her voice sounded in Larry's ears like a peal of bells. He came nearer to the brasier on tiptoe so that the watchman would not perceive him.

"Do you want tea?" the watchman asked sourly.

"Well, you are a perfect gentleman," the woman's voice went on with a laugh. "Nice way to speak to a lady!"

"Oh, I know the sort of a lady you are!" the watchman grumbled.

"Squinty!" and now her voice sounded caressing. "Are you really sore because I left you down the other night? I was sorry, Squinty, honest to God I was, but he was a real nice fella' with tons of dough, and he wanted me so bad!"

Larry, fascinated by the mysterious woman, drew nearer and nearer to the circle of light.

"It isn't only the other night," the watchman snarled. "It's every night. You can't see a man but you want to go off with him. I warn you, my girl——"

But his girl was no longer listening to him.

"Who's that?" she whispered sharply, peering into the shadows where Larry's boyish face was half-hidden.

"Blast you!" shouted the watchman furiously. "Aren't you gone yet?"

The woman strode across to where Larry stood and caught him by the arm. He tried to draw back, but she pulled him into the light of the brasier.

"I say, kid," she said, "aren't you bashful? Let's have a look at you! . . . Why, he's a real beauty, that's what he is."

"I'll splinter his beauty for him in wan minit if he don't get out of this!" the watchman cried. "I'll settle him. He have the heart played out of me this night already."

"Ah, be quiet, Squinty!" said the woman appeasingly.

"I'll be the death of him!"

"No, you won't. . . . Don't you be afraid of him, kid. He's not as bad as he sounds. . . . Make a drop of tea for him, Squinty, the poor kid's hands are freezing."

"I won't make tea for him. I have no liquors to spare for young ragamuffins and sleepouts."

"Aah, do as you're told!" the woman said disgustedly.

"You know there's only two ponnies," said the watchman, subsiding.

"Well, him and me'll drink out of the one. Won't we kid?"

And with amazing coolness she put him sitting on an improvised bench before the fire, sat close beside him, and drew his hand comfortingly about her slender waist. Larry held it shyly; for the moment he wasn't even certain that he might lawfully hold it at all. He looked at this magical creature in the same shy way. She had a diminutive face, coloured a ghostly white, and crimson lips that looked fine in the firelight. She was perfumed, too, with a scent that he found overpowering and sweet. There was something magical and compelling about her. And stranger than all, the watchman had fallen under her spell. He brewed the tea and poured it out into two ponnies, grumbling to himself the while.

"You *know* he have no right to set down there," he was saying. "Nice trouble I'd be getting into if someone came along and seen a . . . seen a woman of the streets and a young reformatory school brat settin' be the fire. . . . Eh, me lady? . . . Oh, very well, very well. . . . This'll be put a stop to, this can't go on forever. . . . And you think I don't know what you're up to, huh? Hm? No, no, my dear, you can't fool an old soldier like me that way. This'll be put a stop to."

"What are you saying, Squinty?" the woman asked.

"Oh, don't mind me! Don't mind me!" The watchman laughed bitterly. "I don't count, but all the same this'll be put a stop to . . . there's your tea!"

He handed her one of the ponnies, then retreated into his watch box with the second. Inside he fumbled in his pockets, removed a little parcel of bread and butter, and tossed her half, which she deftly caught and shared with Larry. Larry had begun to feel that miracles were a very ordinary thing after all.

"Get outside that, kid," she said kindly to Larry, handing him the ponny of boiling tea. "'Twill warm up your insides. What happened you to be out so late? Kissed the girl and lost the tram?"

"Me ould fella –" said Larry, sipping and chewing, "me ould fella' – locked me out!" "Bad luck to him!" he added with a startling new courage.

"Oh, ay, oh, ay!" commented the watchman bitterly from his box. "That's the way they speaks of their fathers nowadays! No respect for age or anything else. Better fed than taught."

"Never mind him, darling," said the woman consolingly. "He's old-fashioned, that's what he is!"

Then as Larry made a frightened sign to her, she laughed.

"Are you afraid he'll hear me? Oh, Squinty doesn't mind a bit. We're old friends. He know quite well what I think of him – don't you, Squinty?" Her voice dropped to a thrilling whisper, and her hand fondled Larry's knee in a

194

way that sent a shiver of pleasure through him. "Will you come home with me, darling?" she asked, without listening to the watchman's reply.

"Oh, I know, I know," the latter answered. "Nice name this place'll be getting with you and all the immoral men and boys of the city making your rondeyvoos here. Sailors . . . tramps . . . reformatory school brats . . . all sorts and conditions. This'll be put a stop to, my lady. Mark my words, this'll be put a stop to. I know what you're saying, I know what you're whispering. It's no use, my dear. You can't deceive me."

"I was only asking him if he'd e'er a place to stop."

"And what is it to you if he haven't, my lady?"

"God help us, you wouldn't like your own son to be out here all night, catching his death of cold or maybe dropping asleep and falling stupid in the fire."

"I wouldn't like me own son to be connaisseuring with the likes of you either."

"He might meet with worse," said the woman, bridling up.

"And where would you bring him?"

"Never mind where I'd bring him! I'd bring him a place he'd be welcome in anyway, not like here."

The watchman suddenly changed his tone, becoming violent, and at the same time conciliatory.

"You wouldn't leave me here lonesome by meself after all you promised me?" he cried.

"I won't remain here to be insulted either."

"He can stay, he can stay," said the watchman submissively. "I won't say a cross word to him."

"He'd rather go home with me," said the woman. "Wouldn't you, darling?"

"I would," said Larry decisively.

"Don't you go! Don't you go, young fellow!" shouted the watchman. "She's an immoral woman. . . . Oh, you low creature," he continued, "aren't you ashamed of yourself? Leaving me lonesome night after night, and chasing off with any stranger that comes the way. Last time it was the dandy fellow off the Swedish boat, and now it's a common brat that his own father won't leave in."

"Now, now, don't be snotty!" said the young woman reprovingly. "It's not becoming to your years. And if you're good maybe I'll come round and see you tomorrow night."

"You'll say that and not mean a word of it!" exclaimed the watchman. "Oh, you low creature. You haven't a spark of honour or decency."

"Come on home, darling, before he loses his temper," said the woman good-humouredly. She rose and took Larry's hand, and with a loud "Good-bye" to the watchman, guided him on to the roadway. As she did so there came the sound of heavy footsteps thudding along the wooden jetty. The woman started nervously and pushed Larry before her towards the shadow of the timber.

"Here, kid," she whispered, "we'll go round by the timbers and up the Park. Hurry! Hurry! I hear someone coming.

The steps drew nearer, and suddenly she dropped Larry's hand and crouched back into the shadows. He heard a quick, stifled cry that terrified him.

"Oh, Sacred Heart, he seen me!" she said, and then in a tense, vicious whisper she cried to the unseen, "May the divil in hell melt and blind you, you clumsy Tipperary lout!"

"Is that you I seen, Molly?" a jovial voice called from the darkness, and a moment later Larry saw the glint of the fire on an array of silver buttons.

"Yes, constable, it's me," the woman answered, and Larry could scarcely recognise her voice for the moment, it was so unctuous, so caressing. But again came the fierce mutter beside him, "Bad luck and end to you, y'ould ram, what divil's notion took you to come this way tonight?"

"Are you alone?" the policeman asked, emerging from the shadows.

"No constable," she sniggered.

"Is there someone with you?"

196

"Yes, constable . . . a friend."

"Oh, a friend, is there? And what's your friend doing out at this hour of the night?" He strode across to Larry and shook his arm. "So you're the friend, me young hopeful? And what have you here at this hour of the night, huh?"

"He was seeing me home, constable, and I took a bit of a weakness so we sat here a while with Squinty."

"Answer me!" thundered the policeman to Larry. "And don't try to tell any lies. What have you out at this hour?"

"Me father" – gasped Larry, "me father – locked me out – sir."

"Mmmm. Your father locked you out, did he? Well, I'm thinking it wouldn't do you any harm to lock you in, d'you hear? How would you like that, eh?"

"Bah!" grunted the watchman.

"What did you say, Squinty?"

"I said right, constable. Right every time! If I'd me way with that sort of young fellow I'd make drisheens of his hide."

"And what about you, Molly?"

"He's a friend of mine, constable," the woman said ingratiatingly. "Let him go now and he won't do it again. I'm finding him a place to sleep – the poor child is perished with the cold. Leave him to me, constable. I'll look after him for the night."

"Aisy now, aisy!" the policeman interrupted heavily. "We're all friends, aren't we?"

"Yes, constable."

"And we want to do the best we can by one another, don't we?"

"Yes, constable."

"I've a word to say to you, so I think I'll take your advice and let the boy go. Squinty will keep an eye on him, won't you, Squinty?"

"You may swear I'll keep an eye on him," the watchman said viciously.

"That's all right then. Are you satisfied now, Molly?"

"Yes, constable," she said between her teeth.

"The same place?"

"Yes, constable."

She turned on her heel and went off slowly along the quay. The darkness was thinning. A faint brightness came from above the hill at the other side of the river. The policeman glanced at it and sighed.

"Well, it's a fine day, thanks be to God," he said. "I had a quiet night of it, and after this I'll have a grand sleep for myself. Will you try a drop, Squinty?"

"I will then," said the watchman greedily.

The policeman took a flask from his pocket and drank from it. He handed it to the watchman, who took another swig and gave it back to him. The policeman held it up to the fire. He closed his left eye and whistled brightly for a few moments.

"There's a *taoscán* in it still," he commented. "I suppose you don't drink, young fellow?"

"I don't," said Larry sourly, "but I'd drink it now if you'd give it to me."

"I will, I will," said the policeman laughing. "And I after taking your girl from you and all. 'Tis the least I might do. But never mind, young fellow. There's plenty more where she came from."

Larry choked over a mouthful of the neat whiskey and handed back the empty flask. The policeman drew out a packet of cheap cigarettes and held it towards him.

"Wish me luck!" he said.

"Good luck!" said Larry, taking a cigarette.

"Fathers are a curse anyway," said the other confidentially. "But I musn't be keeping me little pusher waiting. So long, men."

"So long," said Larry and the watchman together.

The policeman disappeared between the high walls of timber, and Larry sat by the brasier and recklessly lit his cigarette. The watchman, too, lit his pipe, and smoked silently and contentedly, spitting now and again out of sheer satisfaction. The faint brightness over the hill showed

198

clearer and clearer, until at last the boy could distinguish the dim outlines of riverside and ships and masts. He shivered. The air seemed to have become colder. The watchman began to mumble complacently to himself within his box.

"Ah, dear me," he said, launching a spit in the direction of the brasier, "dear me, honesty is the best policy. . . . Yes, my lady, honesty is the best policy after all, that's what I say. . . . I told you I'd (spit) put a stop to your goings-on, my lady; your (spit) Swedish skippers and your dandy boys, and now you're quiet enough, my lady. . . . Now you're quiet enough."

Larry rose.

"Where are you going now?" asked the watchman sourly.

"I'm going home," said Larry.

"Stop where you are now! Didn't you hear what the policeman said?"

"I don't care what the policeman said. I'm going home."

"Home? Aren't you afraid?"

"What would I be afraid of?" asked Larry contemptuously.

"Ah, my boy," said the watchman with fierce satisfaction, "your old fella' will hammer hell out of you when he gets you inside the door!"

"Will he?" asked Larry. "Will he now? I'd bloody well like to see him try it."

And whistling jauntily, he went off in the direction of the city.

POOLBEG

Truth in the Night

Michael McLaverty

In *Truth in the Night,* considered by many to be his finest novel, Michael McLaverty returns to Rathlin Island, the scene of part of his first book, *Call My Brother Back.* Whereas in that book the island is seen with the uncritical eye of a child, here it is viewed more realistically. Although its beauty is evocatively portrayed, life on the island is clearly hard – too hard for some people: the Craigs, who soon abandon it for Belfast; and Vera Reilly, the sharp-tongued unhappy mainland woman, widowed with one daughter who longs to leave. The story of her second marriage to Martin Gallagher, a native of the island whose return after a long absence signifies the fulfilment of a lifelong dream, is told with compassion but unflinching realism.

The character of a tightly-knit rural community, with its concern for its own and suspicion of the stranger, is magnificently conveyed. Rarely in a novel has the redemptive power of love been more manifest.

ISBN 0 905169 72 7

Rep of Irl IR£3.95
UK£3.45

POOLBEG

Dublin 4
Maeve Binchy

By the best selling author of
Light a Penny Candle and *Echoes*.

These four stories, set in the heart of Dublin's fashionable
Southside, focus on the dilemmas facing four ordinary
people. There is a society hostess who invites her
husband's mistress to dinner, a country girl lost in the big
city, a reformed drinker beset by temptations, and a
student grappling with the problem of an unplanned
pregnancy. With her intimate grasp of human feelings
and her uncanny ear for dialogue, Maeve Binchy lavishes
sympathy on all her characters, brave and foolish alike.

ISBN 0 905169 77 8

Rep of Irl IR£3.50
UK£3.15

POOLBEG

Irish Sagas and Folk Tales

Eileen O'Faoláin

Here is a classic collection of tales from the folklore of Ireland. It begins with the heroic sagas, the ancestral tales of men and gods: *The Children of Lir; The Cattle-Raid of Cooley* (the story of the Táin) and *The Fate of the Sons of Usnach*. Then come the stirring tales of Finn and the Fianna, that immortal band of warrior athletes. Finally there are the chimney-corner tales of the Little People – *The Black Thief, The Bird of the Golden Land,* and many others.

Some of these enchanting stories are told in the very words of the countrymen from whom they were first taken down. Throughout the book, Eileen O'Faoláin maintains a fine command of beautiful, flowing language which captures the heart of Irish story-telling at its imaginative best.

ISBN 0 905169 71 9

Rep of Irl IR£3.95
UK£3.45